Dirty Filthy Billionaire

Also From Laurelin Paige

Brutal Billionaires
Brutal Billionaire

Man in Charge Duet
Man in Charge
Man in Love
Man for Me: A Man in Charge Novella (1001 Dark Nights)

Slay Series
Slay One: Rivalry
Slay Two: Ruin
Slay Three: Revenge
Slay Four: Rising
Slash: A Slay Novella (1001 Dark Nights)

The Fixed Series
Fixed on You
Found in You
Forever with You
Hudson
Falling Under You: A Fixed Trilogy Novella (1001 Dark Nights)
Chandler
Dirty, Filthy Fix: A Fixed Trilogy Novella (1001 Dark Nights)
Fixed Forever

Dirty Universe
Dirty Filthy Rich Boys
Dirty Filthy Rich Men
Dirty Filthy Rich Love
Dirty, Sexy Player
Dirty Sexy Games
Sweet Liar
Sweet Fate
Dirty Sweet Valentine
Wild Rebel

Wild War
Wild Heart
Kincaid
Dirty Filthy Billionaire: A Dirty Universe Novella (1001 Dark Nights)

Found Duet
Free Me
Find Me
The Open Door: A Found Duet Novella (1001 Dark Nights)

First and Last
First Touch
Last Kiss

Hollywood Heat
Sex Symbol
Star Struck
One More Time
Close

Co-Written Works:
Written with Sierra Simone:
Porn Star
Hot Cop

Written with Kayti McGee:
Dating Season
Spring Fling
Summer Rebound
Fall Hard
Winter Bloom
Spring Fever
Summer Lovin

Miss Match
Love Struck
MisTaken: A Novella

Dirty Filthy Billionaire
A Dirty Universe Novella
By Laurelin Paige

1001 DARK NIGHTS
PRESS

Dirty Filthy Billionaire
A Dirty Universe Novella
By Laurelin Paige

1001 Dark Nights
Copyright 2023 Laurelin Paige
ISBN: 979-8-88542-015-0

Foreword: Copyright 2014 M. J. Rose

Published by 1001 Dark Nights Press, an imprint of Evil Eye Concepts, Incorporated

Dedication

For all the prickly people who say they hate everyone, so no one knows they have a gooey, vulnerable center

One Thousand and One Dark Nights

Once upon a time, in the future…

*I was a student fascinated with stories and learning.
I studied philosophy, poetry, history, the occult, and
the art and science of love and magic. I had a vast
library at my father's home and collected thousands
of volumes of fantastic tales.*

*I learned all about ancient races and bygone
times. About myths and legends and dreams of all
people through the millennium. And the more I read
the stronger my imagination grew until I discovered
that I was able to travel into the stories… to actually
become part of them.*

*I wish I could say that I listened to my teacher
and respected my gift, as I ought to have. If I had, I
would not be telling you this tale now.
But I was foolhardy and confused, showing off
with bravery.*

*One afternoon, curious about the myth of the
Arabian Nights, I traveled back to ancient Persia to
see for myself if it was true that every day Shahryar
(Persian: شهريار, "king") married a new virgin, and then
sent yesterday's wife to be beheaded. It was written
and I had read that by the time he met Scheherazade,
the vizier's daughter, he'd killed one thousand
women.*

Something went wrong with my efforts. I arrived in the midst of the story and somehow exchanged places with Scheherazade – a phenomena that had never occurred before and that still to this day, I cannot explain.

Now I am trapped in that ancient past. I have taken on Scheherazade's life and the only way I can protect myself and stay alive is to do what she did to protect herself and stay alive.

Every night the King calls for me and listens as I spin tales. And when the evening ends and dawn breaks, I stop at a point that leaves him breathless and yearning for more. And so the King spares my life for one more day, so that he might hear the rest of my dark tale.

As soon as I finish a story... I begin a new one... like the one that you, dear reader, have before you now.

Chapter One

I have one word for the menu in front of me—*fandamntastic*.

Honestly, I'm not surprised. The Annual Awards for Advances in the Media has the best dinner of the year. I should know because I attend many. Every time my boss, Donovan Kincaid, declines an invitation, I RSVP in his place because, seriously. Saffron crème brûlée? Sure beats the from-the-box cheesecake at Doug's Diner on 34th.

Not knocking Doug. He makes most of my meals these days—or his kitchen staff does—but the convenience and affordability rank higher than the taste. He's open late, does take-out and delivery, and is only a block from my apartment. Plus, he lets me order off-menu, which is not easy to find these days.

And again, by *he*, I mean *the staff*. Doug doesn't know me from Eve, and still he's the number one man in my life after Donovan.

That probably says more about me than I should admit.

Point being, I will take any chance I can to get a fancy meal for one that doesn't require a date or using my own credit card. Particularly, when the meal has a dessert as scrumptious as saffron crème brûlée.

I'm already salivating when someone sits in the seat next to me.

This is a good time to mention that I'm not really a people person. Or rather, I'm a specific-people sort of person, meaning I can list the specific people I like on one hand:

1. Donovan.

2. His business partners, Nate and Cade (thank God Weston moved to France because ew).

3. My neighbor Ashish, who waters my plants for me when I need him to. (I return the favor with fairly satisfying casual sex).

4. And Doug of Doug's Diner, whom I've never met and might not even be a real person.

I like my sister, Danelle, most of the time too, but not enough to add her to the list, and besides, family shouldn't count.

It's perhaps a bad quality for someone who has a people-facing job, I know, but I'm pretty good at faking it when I have to. I've never had any of Donovan's clients lodge a formal complaint, and as his capital P, Personal, capital A, Assistant—do not call me secretary; I loathe the word—I interact with all of them. Whatever I lack in customer service, I more than make up for with my organization skills. I know how to hide the dead bodies, so to speak, and Donovan has more of those than many of the other rich bastards in this town.

All that to say, I do not come to these functions to socialize.

Obviously, I RSVP'd a plus one, which means that my purse is occupying the seat to my left. We're given our table number at check-in, so I couldn't do a speedy online stalk of whoever else is assigned to this round. So far, it's been tolerable. The older couple across from me are too uptight to engage with anyone ambiguously ethnic. My straight dark hair and light eyes skew more toward my Brazilian Swiss side, but my darker skin, luscious lips, and bone structure give away my Afro-Japanese genes, so I'm doubting the older couple will try to engage. The couple next to them are fellow Millennials and too into posting on Instagram to have noticed me. The Latina next to them seems to be part of their party. I was prepared to ignore whoever sat in the last empty seat to my right, expecting the usual too white, too old, too out-of-touch misogynist to take the spot.

I am *not* prepared for the six-foot, beardy, dark blond, green-eyed masterpiece that wears a tux better than I wear a grudge—and I'm a Scorpio; I can seriously wear a grudge—that sits beside me. So not prepared that I literally choke on my water.

Thankfully, I'm smooth, and cover it up with a swerve of my head in the opposite direction, along with a subtle cough that I'm sure comes off as a reaction to the circulated air. There's no way he notices.

"Are you okay, there?" Fuck, his voice is sandpaper. The best of all kinds of voices. "If you need the Heimlich, I'm going to have to pass."

I almost choke again for a multitude of reasons:

1. He noticed.

2. That voice.

3. He's going to *pass*?

I gather myself as quickly as possible, which is pretty quick. It's amazing how together I can be when I'm annoyed. "You can't pass on someone choking. What if I'd been dying?"

He looks at me like I'm an idiot. "You weren't dying."

"But what if I had been? You can't just say pass."

He leans an elbow on the table and holds up a single finger. "One, it's not my obligation to know how to do the Heimlich."

Oh my God, he's using lists. That's my language.

His second finger goes up. "Two, it's not my responsibility to attempt to rescue a stranger who would probably sue me for manhandling." A third finger. "Three, nothing's been served but water." He drops his hand, not bothering with holding up another digit. "Four, you're talking to me. You're obviously fine."

So conceited. Obviously an Aries.

Dammit, that makes him even hotter.

I narrow my eyes, unsure if I should bother with a comeback. On the one hand, I don't want to encourage conversation. On the other hand, I do love a good sparring match. Especially if it's followed up with a one-night only tussle in the bedroom. Preferably, *his* bedroom, since my sheets are due for the laundry.

In the end, I can't help myself. No one will ever call Simone Lima a quitter.

I lower my voice so as not to invite the others into the conversation before speaking. "Maybe I popped a cough drop in my mouth."

He leans in, lowering his voice to match mine. "But you didn't."

"But you didn't know that."

"But I did."

"How? You just sat down."

"Because I've been watching you for the past ten minutes."

I'm momentarily speechless. *Point to him.*

When I find my voice, all I'm able to say is, "Oh." Then again, "Ohhhh," drawing out the sound this time, because I see the game now. This is definitely foreplay, and I'm here for it.

Sitting back in my chair, I cross my arms under my breasts, giving them a little needed perk. (They don't need much.) Then I layer my best purr under my words. "Looking for anything particular during your cross-the-room stalking?"

"Honestly? I was trying to decide if the dinner was worth it, or if I should continue schmoozing in the lounge instead."

I'm guessing the reason he chose the meal was moi, but I play coy. "The dinner is definitely worth it."

He shrugs. "Possibly. Worth it enough to have to put up with conversation with strangers?"

God, I've never felt so seen.

It's the exact same question I ask myself every time I decide to attend one of these events. Several invites get tossed immediately after having discovered from experience how not worth conversation with strangers the meals are.

But just as I'm about to express the feeling of kinship, I see that the man has picked up his phone and appears to be scrolling mindlessly.

In other words, the "strangers" he wants to avoid are me.

"You have some nerve." What I really want to say is fuck you, but I don't want to give him the satisfaction of seeing just how riled up I am. "You talked to me first."

"Only because you were trying to get my attention with that fake choking thing, and I wanted you to know that it wasn't going to work."

For fuck's sake. "One"—I hold up a finger as he did just a few minutes ago to me—"I wasn't faking. Two, check your ego, why don't you. Three, if it had been a scheme, it did work, because you haven't paid attention to much of anything but me since you sat down."

"That wasn't faking?" Of all the things I said for him to zero down on. "Are you just awkward or…?"

What I am is about ready to throw my knife at him, but I know I'll need it for the steak tartare. "I was shocked, you narcissist."

"Shocked by…?"

I'm so worked up, I almost blurt out the truth and tell him I was shocked by how attractive he is. Fortunately, I catch myself in time. "Never mind. It's not important."

"No, I'm interested. Please, tell."

His eyes have flecks of blue in the green, I realize. They're mesmerizing, which only makes me more annoyed. "It's none of your business," I say, curtly.

Thankfully, the waiters are coming round now, and a glorious caprese salad is placed in front of me. I'm talking chef's kiss appearance here. I can already taste how good it is.

I cut into the tomato and mozzarella, preparing for my first bite, when Mr. Irritating decides to continue his train-of-thought.

"I had just sat down. Did it have to do with me?" He pauses from slicing into his salad and lifts a tomato-clung fork toward me. "Were you shocked that I was so dashing?"

Just like that, my first sublime bite is ruined.

There must be a god, though, because I flush, but don't choke.

I set down my fork. "I'm shocked that you'd use the word *dashing*. Are you British all of a sudden or did you just age forty years?"

"Denial and misdirection. Obviously, it *was* me."

"Oh, please. I was shocked that anyone could be so arrogant. I could feel it rolling off you before you even opened your mouth." I feel good about that save. "Frankly, men who look as good as you are always assholes. I shouldn't have been surprised."

"Aha! You do think I'm good-looking."

Goddammit.

It's out in the open now. Further denial will only help dig my grave. "You know you're good-looking." Somewhere along the way, my voice has risen to a level that attracts the third wheel of the trio. I decide to make use of her attention. "Is he or is he not irrefutably good-looking?"

She looks to both sides before determining that I am indeed talking to her. "Instagrammable, for sure."

"See?"

But the annoying prick takes advantage of my witness and cross-examines. "Shockingly good-looking?"

"That's an accurate description," she says, and fuck her because now her friends are involved and they both agree.

Mr. Irritating smirks like he knows it's my kryptonite and is intentionally trying to wound me. "I rest my case."

This is why I only like five people.

"Whatever, your 'case'. Like I'm on trial. I swallowed my water wrong, okay? That's all it was. Make nothing more of it." I stab my fork into my tomato so hard that the table shakes and of course the rose bouquet centerpiece topples because that's exactly the way this meal is going.

The ass at my side reaches for it at the same time I do. He manages to save it before water spills everywhere. I manage to snag my finger on a thorn, and now I'm bleeding.

"I hate everything," I mumble, before sticking my finger in my mouth.

"Careful not to choke."

No "are you okay?" or "let me help you with that." I'm not as surprised as I am disappointed because I'm still ridiculously attracted to this jackass. He evokes dirty thoughts, whether I want him to or not, and after I take my finger out and wrap my napkin around it, those thoughts shade my next words. "For your information, I only choke on water."

His eyes darken with undeniable desire. *Point to me.*

But although there are a million and one innuendos that would perfectly land, he takes things in a completely different direction. "Who are you here with?"

I glance at the empty chair at my side.

"Not who came with you. Obviously, you're alone." He doesn't even give me a chance to be offended. "I mean, what organization? What company?"

There's a sinking in my chest, and I'm suddenly sure he's on to me. That he knows somehow that I don't belong here. "What company are *you* with?"

"I asked first."

"I don't care who asked—"

He cuts me off, seemingly not interested in dragging this out. "Sebastian News Corp. Now you."

Sebastian? He's probably just an employee, and not one of the actual Sebastians, but there has been a Holt Sebastian harassing Donovan at work the last couple of weeks. If he's the same guy…

I don't have time to dwell on that because he's waiting for my answer. It makes the most sense to admit I'm with *Reach* marketing, especially because Donovan's wife is here as a presenter somewhere. We're too far from the stage to be worried that she'll see me, but it would be just my luck that this guy would talk to her and mention me.

And Sabrina's such a goody-two shoes that there's no way she won't make a big deal about it.

Besides, if this *is* the same guy harassing Donovan, or connected to him, then there's a good chance my presence here will get reported back to my boss directly.

So instead, I blurt the first name that comes to mind. "I'm a personal assistant with Pierce Industries."

"Hudson?"

"Mm hm." I stuff another bite of salad in my mouth.

"Trish isn't working with him anymore?"

Of course he fucking knows Hudson Pierce's secretary.

I set my fork down and take a swallow—a *careful* swallow—of my water before answering. "I thought you were asking if Hudson was the Pierce of Pierce Industries. Which he is. I'm not his personal assistant."

"Then whose personal assistant are you?"

I should make up a name, but for some reason I'm not thinking as clearly as usual. It's like half of my blood has traveled south—damn him for being as hot as he is annoying—so I'm not at my best when I say, "Chandler's."

I'm an idiot.

It's the second worst answer I could have given after Hudson, because he's Hudson's little brother and almost as well-known. In fact, Chandler is really involved with the media aspect of Pierce Industries, and there's a fairly good chance he's here tonight.

So when Mr. Shockingly Irritating opens his mouth to say something that will likely pin me further in my grave, I grab my purse and stand. "Actually, I think I'm at the wrong table."

As fast as I can, I head out of the ballroom, just as the first presenter takes the stage. The round of applause that bursts as I open the door couldn't have been better scripted. I escaped. I deserve the acclaim.

But then I hear my name called out from across the lobby. "Simone."

Karma must have finally caught up with me because when I lock eyes on the person who spoke, it's none other than my boss, Donovan Kincaid.

Chapter Two

Here's the thing—will Donovan fire me for using his discarded invites without his permission? No.

Will he reprimand me? Also, no.

Will he take advantage of my desire to attend these functions and put me to work at future events? No, probably not.

In fact, he'd probably pat me on the back while giving me one of his infamous smirks and tell me how to get a hold of his partners' discarded invites as well. Donovan and I are two of a kind like that, which is the real reason he keeps me around, not my awesome PA skills. It's not always easy to find company while walking semi-ethical lines.

But this is *my* thing. My thing that has nothing at all to do with who I am during office hours. It's personal and private and sort of embarrassing, when I think about admitting it out loud, because it's not just about getting free food. Hell's Kitchen apartments take a fair amount of my salary, but Donovan pays well. I can afford to go out.

I just don't really want to go eat solo in expensive restaurants.

People stare and whisper. Not that I care what they think, but it's distracting. It's much easier to be a solo at a business function. Maybe my plus one is involved in the actual event. Maybe they canceled, last minute. Maybe I'm there purely because of work, and no one whispers or stares or judges, and waiters don't give me pitying comments, and strange men don't (usually) take it as an opportunity to hit on me.

It's a perfect hobby, as far as I'm concerned, and I'll be damned if it's taken away because of the hazel-eyed assface who sat at my table, who is the sole reason I'm out in the lobby at the same time Donovan is.

I have half a mind to turn around and go tear that too-hot-for-his-own-good fucker to shreds, and I would if my boss wasn't looking at me like I'm a lifeline.

I quickly try to make up a backstory. "Uh, Donovan…I'm…" Try and fail. "Hi. You're here."

He waves to a security guard then points at me, which…okay. Maybe I was wrong thinking he wouldn't be mad. He really doesn't have to go so far as to bring security in.

But though the guard is eyeing us, he doesn't make a move, letting Donovan approach me.

"Hey, I'm looking for Sabrina. Do you…?" Donovan trails off, and I can see that I misjudged the situation, because it's just now that his expression becomes suspicious. "What are you doing here? Did you use my ticket?"

"No!" The denial was too obvious, but I've chosen my path. Now I have to walk it. "No. Of course I didn't do that. I just. I'm, um, here—"

Suddenly, an arm slips around my waist. "She's here with me. It's okay, Simone. We don't have to keep it a secret."

I look up to see it's none-other-than the antagonizing prick from the ballroom, and I'm both shocked and…aroused?

I mean, I'm not into being rescued. By anyone. Ever.

Especially not by strangers that I want to punch in the face. But his hand feels warm around my body, and there's definitely some action happening in my lower parts. Even as it occurs to me that this rescue will most likely come at a cost. A steep cost, I'm betting.

And godfuckingdammit, he heard Donovan say my name. He's going to use it like a weapon, now. I know it.

It takes Donovan only two seconds to size him up. "You're a Sebastian."

"Steele," he says, offering his free hand to Donovan. "And you are?"

Oh, shit. An actual Sebastian, not just someone who works for the company. No wonder he's so arrogant.

Though, his elitist tone makes my insides turn to jelly. I've always known my place on the hierarchy, which is below anyone with the name Kincaid. With a Sebastian's arm around me, I'm automatically moved up the ladder to a position at least equal to, if not higher than, the man in front of me.

Donovan doesn't seem to like it one bit.

He takes the offered hand and narrows his eyes with irritation, presumably because he has to announce his name. "Donovan Kincaid."

If I know him at all—and I do—I'm sure he's squeezing Steele's hand extra hard.

Fun as it is to be wrapped up in this pissing contest, I know where my loyalty lies. "That's my boss, Steele. Honey." I add the final word last minute, cringing at how awkward it feels in my mouth. "Be nice."

"Ah, right. Your boss. At that advertising agency you work at."

"Uh-huh." I try to smile, but it's forced because I've obviously made a big error in judgment. As soon as Mr. Arrogant—Steele, I guess—put his arm around me, I should have given up the ghost and confessed to Donovan.

Now, I'm on the wrong side of a billionaire battle. Steele is smooth, and apparently at least knows *of* Donovan, by name, if not by face, and all of that makes me nervous. What will he expect in exchange for this favor? If I'm going to be swimming with sharks, I'd much rather be with the shark I know.

Wouldn't I?

Before I can doubt myself to the point of confession, Donovan switches gears. "Yeah, yeah, nice meeting you. Hey, Simone, I left my ticket at the office, and I can't get inside without it."

I don't feel guilty, exactly. It's his fault for telling me to decline his RSVP. "If I'd known you were—"

He cuts me off. "I wasn't planning on coming, Just something came up, and I need to talk to Sabrina, but this fine lady"—he smiles toward the host who is watching us from the check-in desk—"won't let me in without a ticket."

As if to prove her point, she calls out. "Still can't let you in."

"You need me to get you in?" Steele offers, as if he's better at pulling strings than Donovan Kincaid.

Okay, maybe he is, and if so then…hot. (Sigh).

"No," Donovan says sharply. "Thank you. I just need Simone to try to find her for me, have her come out for a second."

Something is wrong.

I should have sensed it immediately, but I was too distracted by…well, things that shouldn't have distracted me. Donovan doesn't show up at events like this, spur-of-the-moment. He doesn't drop subjects when he has a bone to pick. He doesn't speak with the sense of urgency that I hear now in his tone.

He's obsessed with his wife, Sabrina, but he doesn't bring me into dealing with her. Something's up. "An emergency?"

"Not an emergency. But important. And urgent. But not anything to worry about. Make sure she's not worried."

Yeah, definitely an emergency.

"Uh, sure." I look toward Steele, as though he might be helpful, who knows why. "I'm not sure where the presenters are seated…"

"In the front, sweetie." The endearment rolls off his tongue easier than it did mine, sending goosebumps down my arms. "Do you want me to come with you?"

"No." If this really is urgent, I don't need more of his distraction. "I've got it."

It's not until I'm halfway to the ballroom that I realize I chose wrong, again. What was I thinking, leaving Steele with my boss? If he's not ratting me out, he's probably gathering more information from Donovan to use against me. Thankfully, Donovan is usually good at picking up on other sharks, but he's obviously off tonight. Something's up. Something with Sabrina.

That's what I should be thinking about as I head toward the faux stage, not Steele. I should be focused on whatever has my boss in a tailspin. Admittedly, I'm not that fond of his wife—she pulls a lot of Donovan's attention and always demands special treatment. "Interrupt Donovan from his meeting, please" kind of special treatment. Or "I don't care if he has a full schedule, I need to see him in my office." It's so annoying having lovers in the same office. I have to keep track of her schedule as well as his, think of her time as well as his. It's like pulling double duty.

Like right now. I'm looking for Sabrina when I should be bickering with the arrogant Sebastian in the Brioni suit who looks at me like he might eat me up and makes me feel like I actually might like it.

Fortunately, the stage manager isn't too hard to find. "Pardon me. I work with Sabrina Lind—I mean, Kincaid—and I need to get her a message. Do you know where I can find her?"

The woman seems annoyed at the intrusion until she hears Sabrina's name. "She *was* here. Checked in and everything, but then she left to go to the bathroom or something, and when she came back, she grabbed her purse and rushed out. Before presenting her award."

"Oh, fuck." That's not like goody-goody Sabrina at all. "She didn't tell anyone where she was going?"

The stage manager shrugs. "Sorry. Hope nothing's wrong, but I gotta get back to—" She nods toward the stage.

"Of course. Thank you."

I double my walking speed back to Donovan, and I'm breathless when I'm back in the lobby, noting with dismay that Steele is still there, and that whatever they were talking about has left Donovan somewhat heated.

Why do I have the sinking feeling that it has to do with me?

Remembering my priorities, I concentrate on delivering the news. "She's not here."

Donovan's whole body tenses up. "What do you mean she's not here?"

"I don't know. I talked to the stage manager. Said she was here but she left. Rushed out, actually. Before the award she was supposed to present."

He's concerned, and that makes me concerned.

I'm sure he's thought of this already, but... "You tried to call her?"

His phone is already in his hand. Before he dials, the phone rings. He checks the caller ID before answering. "What happened? Where is she?"

Their driver, Danny, I'm guessing.

I lean in, trying to hear the response. The voice sounds like it's Danny, and while I can't make out everything, I think I hear something about an emergency room.

"Don't leave her side. I'm on my way." When he hangs up, he gives me the bare minimum of details. "New York Presbyterian. I need you to..." He's already walking toward the elevator, so I trot to keep up with his long strides while he tries to articulate what he needs.

I try to guess. "Do you have a ride?"

"I drove."

I'd offer to drive if I knew how, but I've always lived in walking friendly cities and never bothered with a license. "I could call you a cab if you'd rather."

"I'll be faster."

"I'll let the guys know."

"Yes. And Roxie. Have her cancel her, um..." He pushes the elevator call button. When it doesn't open immediately, he presses it several more times in succession. "Have her..."

It's freaky to see my totally-cool-as-a-cucumber boss so rattled. "I'll have Roxie clear Sabrina's schedule for tomorrow. I'll get yours cleared too."

He nods. The elevator opens, and he rushes in, pushing the parking garage button with as much demand as he did the down button.

"Call me if you need anything else," I say as the door shuts.

I'll do what I can, even if he doesn't call. I'm as dependent on my cell as anyone else, but I prefer the tactile feel of a writing instrument in hand so I carry a notepad and pen with me at all times. Spotting a bench along the wall, I pull them both from my purse and head over to it so I can sit and get organized.

After sending a text to Nate and Roxie, I start a to-do list.

1. Call Danny for more info

2. Order dinner for Donovan and Sabrina if they're going to be home tonight

3. Order flowers to be sent to home or hospital

I pause my writing when I feel a presence looming over me. A very manly, dominating, arrogant presence.

A quick glance up, and sure enough, Steele Sebastian is standing there, hands crossed over his chest, his eyes pinned on me, as though waiting for something.

I get it. He rescued me once. He thinks I need rescuing again. As if I don't know how to handle an emergency. "I'm good."

"Except that you owe me."

For fuck's sake, seriously? I'd assumed he'd play this game, but can't he see that I'm busy doing very important assistant things? "I don't have time for you."

I go back to my list, but find it hard to concentrate. *What was the other thing I need to do?*

"That's not how this works." Steele continues to loom.

What I need to do is finish this list elsewhere.

"Not how *what* works? Your privileged life where everyone falls over themselves to please you?" I throw the pen and pad in my purse, then stand. "You might not have ever heard this before, but I have more important things to deal with."

I start toward the elevator, but his voice follows me like a dog with a scent. "That's not how blackmail works." He waits until I turn back to glare before adding, "Simone."

Shit.

My name sounds obscene in his mouth, and paired with the predatory look in his eyes, my knees can barely hold me up. See? Using it like a weapon.

I reach out to the wall, trying to remember words and how they work and what I wanted to say in response.

Ah, yes. "Blackmail? You don't have anything on me."

Somewhat recovered, I resume making my exit.

This time, he follows with more than just his voice. "I do, though. First, I prevented you from having to admit to your boss that you are here with his ticket."

Without turning around, I shake my head, dismissively. If Donovan finds out, he finds out.

"Second, I now know that Kincaid is in the midst of an emergency, something he likely doesn't want revealed to the media before he's ready."

I whirl around to face him. "You wouldn't." Tattling like that about others in the fold is against the billionaire code of conduct, isn't it?

Though, the man's family does own a huge news network and several media outlets…

He shrugs. "I might. The point is, you don't know."

This feels like a repeat of the conversation we had when I'd been choking. It has nowhere to go but round and round, and like I said before, I don't have time.

Before I can turn away a third time, he continues. "Third, you don't know what Donovan and I talked about while you were gone."

Okay, he's got me there. Really got me. He proved he was smooth, and that means that, under the guise of being my boyfriend, he could have lured all sorts of information out of my boss.

But Donovan wouldn't have said anything too terrible. Right?

Right??

"You're bluffing." I finish my trek to the elevator, feeling him hot on my heels.

"You don't know that I'm bluffing."

"Well, I don't care." I hit the down button.

His arm stretches above me to lean on the wall above the call panel, which is…whoa. Sexy. "Now who's bluffing?"

"I'm." I have to clear my throat. "I'm not bluffing." I can't even remember what I'm supposedly bluffing about. All I can think about is how slick my thighs suddenly are, and wondering when I can work self-care into my night's agenda.

"You, Simone, are a bad, bad liar." God, he's such a villain. In the yummiest way.

Fuck. *I don't have time for this!*

I push the button again, repeatedly. When the elevator opens, I'm surprised by the cart full of desserts that rolls out, and I step aside, stupidly bumping into Steele when I do.

My body shivers at the sudden touch, and once more, my knees buckle. This time, he's the one who steadies me. He leans in closer. "Admit it, Simone."

I'm not admitting anything. Certainly not how badly I want to lift my chin and angle my mouth toward his.

I close my eyes, searching for something to anchor me. Something to keep me focused and on task.

Wait…was that cart really full of desserts?

I peek around Steele's body at the cart. It's only a couple of feet away—the man who pushed it out, having abandoned it for the time being to flirt with the check-in lady. It gives me a chance to examine it and see that, yes, indeed, it's a cart full of desserts.

I hadn't even noticed dinner was served.

I missed the damn steak tartare, and it's no one's fault but Steele's.

Anger gives me the force to step away from his magnetic pull. "You rescued me, but you also" — I put up a demonstrative finger — "let me choke." Another finger. "Made me get cut by a rose thorn." Another finger. "And made me miss my dinner." I drop my hand. "I owe you nothing."

Without waiting for his reply, I cross to the cart and swipe a dessert. It's not really swiping since I was supposed to get one anyway, though I wasn't supposed to keep the bowl.

C'est la vie.

I catch the elevator just before the doors close. Steele is still standing there, watching, a curious smirk on his face.

I lift the bowl. "I guess you have this on me now too. Still pretty sure I come out ahead." I push the button for the first floor, and when the doors close and the elevator takes me away from the handsome devil, I feel triumphant.

For all of two seconds.

After which I start to feel the tug of regret. Maybe I should have played along. It won't take me long to do what I need to do for Donovan, and what will I do with the rest of my evening then? I could have made time to "owe" a hot, arrogant billionaire.

Whatever. I hate people.

I have what I truly need to be happy—saffron crème brûlée.

Chapter Three

God, I hate Tuesdays.

Everyone's usually hating on Mondays, but there's always so much to do, who has time for hate? The day goes by in a snap. Yesterday went particularly fast knowing I had the award dinner that night.

Little did I know…

But Tuesdays drag on and on. Especially when the boss is out for who knows how long with a family emergency. I had his whole day rescheduled by nine am. At nine-thirty, he checked in with a phone call saying Sabrina was fine, but they'd both be out for at least the rest of the week.

Donovan rarely likes to show any of his cards, but I tried to peek anyway. "Are you going to tell me what the emergency is?"

"Are you going to tell me what you were doing with Steele Sebastian?"

"Are you going to tell me what he said to you while I was gone?"

"Are you going to tell me why you're concerned about what he might have said?"

Obviously, I had no choice but to fold. "Personal emergency it is. Call if you need me to rework next week too."

I got the rest of the week rescheduled by eleven.

After an early (and long) lunch, I've cleared most of my to-do list, and now the clock says it's only two-fifteen.

What am I supposed to do to fill three more hours?

Yeah, yeah, there's always things to work on, but without Donovan here to glare at me whenever I think of opening a gossip site on my computer—I swear he always knows—I don't have any motivation to find more to be done. Every time I even try to devote myself to a task, I find my mind wandering to Steele Sebastian and his…his…his everything.

Next thing I know, I'm hating the universe for making hot unattainable men and dropping them in my pathway and then giving me so much time to daydream about their eyes and their mouths and their big, big hands…

At two forty, I do an online search and find way too many pictures of the billionaire with way too pretty women on his arm.

At two forty-six, I erase my Google history, because Donovan probably looks at that shit.

At two forty-seven, I repeat the search on my cell phone. I save a couple of the best shots to my favorites folder.

At two fifty-five, I order a new cord for my rechargeable battery.

At two fifty-six, I start to feel ridiculous, so at two fifty-seven, I give up any pretense of working, pop me some low sodium popcorn, and take my curvy ass into Donovan's office so I can watch daytime TV on his couch. With a press of the button that makes his clear glass wall opaque, no one else in the office can see that I'm not working. Not that anyone comes down to this side of the floor when Donovan's gone. It's practically a ghost town. My favorite kind of working environment.

Suddenly, Tuesday isn't feeling quite so revolting.

"Does your boss know this is how you spend his time?"

The unexpected voice jolts me from Dr. Phil's interview with a woman who claims she's married to Jesus, and I spill popcorn all over the sofa. Instinctually, I jump to clean it up and plead my defense, when I realize who the voice belongs to.

Steele fucking Sebastian.

I ignore the trip of my traitor heart—I'm having words with her later—and put on my best bored expression. "Does *your* boss know how you spend *his* time?"

He leans against the doorway like he owns it. "I'm my own boss."

"Funny. That's not what the internet says." Apparently, my earlier online stalking was useful for more than just gathering inspirational me-time pics. It turns out that Steele Sebastian, billionaire that he may be, isn't the top of the food chain at SNC. He reports to his older brother, Holt. "If I had to report to my sibling, I think I'd just kill myself and get it over with."

The remark doesn't land how I intend because he returns it with a smug smile. "You Googled me?"

Dammit. I'm usually better than rookie moves like that.

Fortunately, I know how to recover. "I find it's best to know your enemy."

"I do too. We're talking biblical sense, right?"

The turn in the conversation catches me off-guard, and I'm left speechless. Also, my nipples are at full mast, if you catch my drift.

I fold my arms over my chest before he gets the idea that I'm into getting dirty with him. I mean, it's not off the table, but I'm definitely annoyed. "Why are you here, Mr. Sebastian?"

"So formal. Does this mean I should be referring to you as Ms. Lima?" He drops my last name as though I'll be surprised he knows it.

"Not impressive when it's literally on the nameplate on the desk behind you."

"I didn't see the nameplate." He steps into the office, closing the door behind him, which sends my pulse into rapid-fire mode.

Rightfully so, because I'm now in close quarters with a stranger, and that's supposed to be alarming. Though, I think my heart is more excited than scared, and I'm not sure what to do with that except internally freak out while he surveys the office, checking out the view, and inspecting Donovan's items like he's silently appraising their value.

"Could you put that—" I start when he picks up a framed picture of Sabrina but cut myself off when I realize he's enjoying needling me. I manage to keep my mouth closed while he continues his assessment, until he opens Donovan's prized possession—his cigar box.

I rush to take it from him and return it to its place on the shelf. "If you don't want to tell me what you're here for, I can always call security."

"You don't need to call anyone." He leans/sits on the back of the sofa, and stares at me. His full attention is like an unexpected bright light, and I have to blink several times before I can meet his gaze.

"So…"

"I came to collect."

I want to roll my eyes, but now that I'm looking at him, it's hard to stop looking at him and the gesture probably looks more like I have dirt in my contact than an eyeroll. "I think I already explained that—"

He cuts me off. "You gave me a list of reasons why you think we're even. Now I'm going to give you a list of reasons why I think we're not. One—you were never choking. Two—you spilled the roses. Three—you might have missed dinner, but you still got the best part. Four—your boss gave me his cell number, and I could text him right now to tell him not only that you used his ticket last night, but that you've also spent your whole day watching soaps in his office."

"Not the whole day," I say, meekly.

Then realizing that wasn't the best answer, I try again. "Talk shows, not soaps."

Wait. That wasn't any better.

Focusing on the part of his statement that is surely a blatant lie, I try once more. "Donovan didn't give you his number."

He shrugs. "Maybe not. Maybe I got it from my brother then."

Fucknugget. He might be telling the truth this time. There's really no way to know.

The thing is, if Donovan finds out either of the things that Steele is hanging over my head, no big deal.

The other thing is I'm pretty sure Steele knows that. He's proven himself too capable. There's no way he doesn't have this figured out.

In other words, this is a no stakes game we're playing. I have nothing to lose except my pride. Which is significant, but worth gambling with. Considering how boring my day was until he showed up, I'm already ahead. Might as well hear his appeal. "What would make us even?"

"Not much. Nothing too painful."

"Stop dragging it out and just tell me what you want."

He stands and crosses toward me, caging me against the bookcase so that I have nowhere to go when he leans down to speak softly at my ear. "Oh, there's an awful lot I want, Simone."

My stomach flips at the rasp of his voice.

"But for us to be even? I need to spank you."

Chapter Four

"You want to…spank me?" It's embarrassing how damp my panties are from the thought.

I swear he knows, too, because his lip curled up in a smirk that definitely says *I know all your secrets, Simone Lima. I know them, and by God I'm going to use every last one of them against you.*

Of course, I sort of believe everyone feels that way, which is only one of the long lists of reasons I'm a people hater.

"You heard me."

"Here? Now?"

"Since I don't trust that you'll show up to any other arranged meeting place or time, yes. Here. Now." It's like he already knows me.

I'm trying to picture it—me, bent over Donovan's desk. "Spank me like I'm a five-year-old caught with her hand in the cookie jar?"

"More like spank you like you're a grown woman, with *my* hand in the cookie jar." Oh my wow. "If that's where spanking leads."

Where else does spanking lead?

Which means this isn't a conversation about spanking. This is a conversation about getting kinky.

Get kinky with a hot billionaire with smoldering eyes? Generally, I'm all for that.

But, but, but…

Warning bells sound in my head for no discernable reason. I'm still trapped between him and the bookcase, though, which turns out to be a very bad thinking spot. Bad reception to the neurons or something like that.

So I slip out from under his arm and don't stop until I'm a couple of yards away in clear-thinking territory.

Ha ha. There's no clear-thinking territory when Steele's in sight, because as soon as I turn to look at him, my knees start to give, and I nearly bend myself over and lift my skirt right then and there.

And now I have another question. "Are you thinking over the panties, or…?"

"Is it even a spanking if it's not skin to skin?"

Yep, yep. I've definitely lost all thought capability. All the blood has rushed to my cookie jar and my head can't possibly reason.

I try to make a mental Why I Shouldn't Allow This list, anyway:

1.

"You're thinking too hard." *Just the opposite, Steele, darling. There is no thinking inside this brain.* "There's nothing to consider. It's not a question."

I blink. "Not a question?"

"You owe me, and I've come to collect. This spanking will happen, regardless of what excuse that gorgeous head of yours comes up with. As a courtesy, I'll give you another ten seconds to get used to the idea, and then, ready or not, I'm coming for you."

Well, damn.

"One," he says, and I take a step back, my heart beating so fast I feel it in my throat. "Two." Another step back, and I bump against Donovan's desk. "Three."

"There are cameras in here!"

"Better not give anyone a reason to have to review them, then. Four."

"You recognize this entire situation is inappropriate and could warrant investigation, don't you?" *Oh my god, it's like I'm trying to stop him.*

"Five."

Apparently, he's not afraid of consequences. Why would he be? His family probably owns the law.

"Six." He takes his first step toward me, and I scurry to the opposite side of the room.

It shouldn't come as a surprise when he smiles. As if he's looking forward to a chase. "Seven."

And now my palms are as wet as my panties.

Seriously, I'm both thrilled and terrified. Ridiculous, I know. There's no real reason to be scared. All I have to do is scream or pick up Donovan's phone, and someone will come running.

But I want this. So I haven't done those things.

Yet, I'm still daunted.

This time when he moves, he's between me and the door. "Eight."

In full disclosure, I'm generally the one who comes on strong. If I want to fuck someone, I make it happen. If I want to be spanked, I tell the guy (or girl; okay, that was mostly in college, aka my experimental years) how many strikes and just how hard. I'm the one behind the driver's wheel. I'm the one who chases or, when I'm in the mood, I'm the one who decides to be chased.

"Nine."

This is new ground for me. I'm not sure how to…

"Ten."

I fake in one direction, then dart in the other, but I'm no match for his speed. In a flash, he has his arm around me.

I yelp as he hoists me over his shoulder. Two steps later, he's seated on the couch with me strewn across his lap, ass in the air, and *oh, yes*. This is a much better position than I imagined. Especially when he strokes his hand over my silk black hair and down my spine.

I shiver and goosebumps grow along my flesh.

He brings his other hand to cuff around my neck, and I almost moan. "All good?"

What a silly question. My nipples are sharp enough to cut through the fabric of my blouse, and I'm so turned on I'm about to start hyperventilating. How could I possibly be all good? "Just get on with it."

Even though I can't see him, I sense the smirk on his face as he flips up my skirt to expose my panties. Every muscle in my body tenses as I momentarily freak out about which pair I put on this morning. I relax when I remember that I found a satin black pair in the back of my drawer so I didn't have to wear the splotchy laundry day ones that I almost put on.

I might have to start going to church if God keeps stepping in like this to help a girl out.

Steele's fingers curl around the waistband of the aforementioned satin black underwear. "Lift your hips."

I do. With a growl. Mad more at myself than him for giving into this scheme so easily.

With one hand—the other is still cuffed tightly at my neck—he shimmies the panties down until they're just below my ass leaving my pussy bare against his thigh. "Very nice," he says, and I purr.

For real, I don't understand the sound that is bubbling in my throat. Like a legit purr.

I cough in an attempt to hide it, forgetting that didn't go so well for me last time.

"Choking again?" He sweeps his hand across my bare skin, and stop myself just before I purr again.

"I was trying to hide my snoring. Snoozefest here, Steele. Are you doing this or what?"

His chuckle reverberates through his body and lights my nervous system on fire. Why does he have to be so infuriatingly sexy? I desperately want to "squirm" so that my clit can find some friction, but I won't give him the satisfaction of knowing how needy I am.

And I am so very, very needy.

"You'll take three," he says.

"*Three?*" I start to twist toward him to see if he's out of his mind, but his hand at my neck holds me in place. "Three isn't a punishment." It's foreplay.

"Any more, and I'm afraid you'll get a wet spot on my suit. It's Brioni."

"Fuck you, with your billionaire Brioni." It appears I now have a favorite designer. "I'm not the one whose jizz you need to worry about." I already feel stirrings beneath me that indicate a rather well endowment in his pants.

And wasn't that the point of this whole encounter? Preferably, we both jizz.

"Doubt it."

"Are you playing a different game than I—" The first strike comes without warning, cutting me off sharply. "What the fucking—"

Before I can manage the string of curse words poised at the tip of my tongue, Steele rubs the sting away with the same palm that delivered the blow. "Oh. Ohhhh."

Maybe I will be the one who comes first.

Steele's voice breaks through my euphoric haze. "One."

"One, what?" Oh, right. "One, one. I got it. I can count, you asshole."

Again, that laugh. Again, my nervous system is lit up.

Refusing to give in and let my body seek relief, I force myself to concentrate on inspecting the wear of the leather, making a mental note to look at getting the couch reupholstered.

After a deep breath and several swirls of his palm across my skin, I'm practically a new woman. "Is that all you—?"

The second smack is harder than the first, and just as unexpected. "Are you kidding me?" Water pricks the corner of my eyes. My pussy cries as well.

I hope I've ruined his precious Brioni.

"Feeling it now, are you?" His hand is already back, already smoothing away the sting.

"Feeling what? Did you do something?" I'm a glutton.

"Cute," he says. "Two."

"Two," I repeat. Already it's almost over, and I'm both afraid I won't be able to sit the rest of the day and worried that one more won't be enough.

On the other hand, the endowment beneath me has grown in size, and if I bite back my pride and sacrifice one more purr—and maybe a little bit of squirming—there's a real good chance he might leak as well.

"Is it too much? Should I stop?"

"No!" Dammit. Too desperate. "Unless you think you can't handle it." I buck my hips grazing my pussy against his thick ridge in an attempt to rile him but end up having to swallow a whimper.

"I'm not put out in the least."

"Then by all means, go—"

He's a master at catching me unaware. The third strike burns hottest, and this time when he soothes it with his palm, he presses hard enough into my skin that my pelvis rocks against that steel rod of his and there is absolutely no way that I can suppress the jagged moan that spills, long and drawn out, from my throat.

"Three," he says.

Three, and I am defeated. Three measly slaps, and I'm a wet puddle of mush, in urgent need of an orgasm.

But now that I've lost, I can admit it and get to the good stuff. I know when surrender is the only way to get what I want, and what I want now is for that brutal hand to make its way into the cookie jar, as promised, and—

Before the thought is finished, I'm thrown off Steele's lap as he stands.

I peer at him from the floor. "What was that?"

"That was three. You're done." He brushes his hand down his thigh, casually inspecting the fabric as though there isn't a bulge between his legs. "A wet spot. I knew you couldn't take it."

He's entirely too smug.

And he's entirely too walking away. "You're leaving?" Without even offering to help me up from the floor?

He gives a purposefully blank look. "We're finished here. I can't think of any reason to stay."

So this is the game. Am I supposed to beg now? Or did he come here wanting to turn me on just so he could leave me with a blue clit and still several hours to go before I have access to my vibrator?

What could he possibly gain from that?

Whatever his motive, I'm not going to beg.

I make my way to my feet, as smoothly as possible, and pull up my panties like a big girl. "Honestly, I'd thought you'd already gone." I pretend to yawn.

"As long as we're on the same page then." With that, he opens the door and leaves.

He leaves.

Really leaves.

I rush to the doorway and call after him. "I bet you leave all the women you're with unsatisfied."

Steele acts like he didn't hear me. Dina, from accounting, on the other hand, gives me a stern look.

Oh, like you don't get it, Dina. That woman has a face that says she hasn't been satisfied in years.

I'm still reeling about Steele and his abrupt departure and the intense buzz between my thighs, when the phone rings, reminding me that I'm actually supposed to be on the clock.

I stomp over to my desk to answer it with a sharp, "Donovan Kincaid's office."

"Holt Sebastian. Can you put him on the line?" Steele walks out and his brother calls right after. Is that a coincidence? Maybe Steele is trying to get to my boss through me. I know Donovan has met with Holt but he's also avoided a lot of his calls.

Whatever the ploy, it gives me intense satisfaction to be able to say that Donovan is unavailable. See? A girl wants to be pleased, she has to do the work herself.

"Yes, my brother said he was out for a family emergency. I thought I'd follow up."

"Well, he's not here. But speaking of your brother…" I start to sit in my desk chair, only to remember my ass has been assaulted, and I quickly stand again. "Do you know how I can get in touch with him?"

Whether or not this will play out in a way that's beneficial to me, I don't know. Worth a shot anyway.

"Steele?" Holt sounds surprised that I'd ask, but not surprised enough to withhold information. He's trying to win Donovan over, after all. "I can get you a line to his assistant, but he's not available today. He's filling in for me at a conference in Boston."

"Oh, really?" Ignoring my ass pain, I sit down and pick up a pen so I can take notes because Mama just hit the jackpot.

Chapter Five

The way to a PA's heart is not, as many think, food—it's information.

A fifteen-minute tutorial on automating email responses is all it takes before Claudette, Steele's (rather young but competent) assistant agrees to slip me into his eleven AM time slot on Wednesday (hump day) morning.

Playing to my strengths, I walk brazenly in his office without knocking, wearing a skirt that shows off my legs, yet isn't too tight to be easily moved out of the way. I purposefully shut the door behind me loud enough to draw attention, but devil that he is, he types for several seconds before he looks up.

And then it's just a glance. "You might lock it, too."

He goes back to typing, and I stand frozen for a beat, teetering between my options. Locking the door means potentially more fun to be had. It also means following his orders, and I'm here on my terms not his.

I leave the door unlocked. "Aren't you going to ask why I'm here?"

He types a few more words, then pushes his keyboard aside, seeming to give me his full attention. "I presume you're here because you can't get enough of me."

"That ego again." He's not wrong, but I'm not admitting it flat out.

He studies me, from head to toe, his eyes darkening when he reaches my legs, and I take that as a point. "Aren't you supposed to be on the clock?"

"Took a personal day." Pretending not to notice how keenly he's scrutinizing me, I survey the office, moseying past his desk as I do to look out the windows. It's a nice office. A decent size with a notable view. "Donovan will be pleased to know his is bigger."

"Are you sure? Maybe we should measure."

I flip my head back toward him. "Your ruler or mine?"

"Definitely mine."

I'm not even sure what we're talking about anymore, but there's absolutely innuendo. The tension is so thick, it could be served on a platter. Then he runs his teeth along his lower lip, and I know I have him. "Ask me why I'm here, Steele."

"Why are you here, Simone?"

A shiver runs through me. Apparently, I'm a switch, because as much as I adored him bossing me around yesterday, I still love when a man does what I say.

I slink toward him and cock my hip against his desk. "You weren't where you were supposed to be yesterday, were you? Your brother called. Said you were supposed to be attending a conference for him when you were harassing me."

A single brow lifts. "Oh, really?" He sounds more intrigued than concerned, but I can work with that.

"No need to worry. I covered for you. But you know what that means."

"That my brother doesn't know how to best use my time?"

I resist a grin. "That you owe me."

"Ah. I owe you." He swivels his chair to face me completely. "You're here to collect, I suppose. What, pray tell, do you need to even the score? I don't imagine that you want to spank me."

The thought had crossed my mind.

Several times, actually.

His clothes suggest a firm ass, and I'd love to have my hand on it. Would love to see if there's any flesh to squeeze. Would love to lick my thumb and work it inside him. Wouldn't it be something if I were the first?

It sounds divine, but I have other ideas to settle this debt.

Boldly, I climb onto his lap, straddling my knees on either side of his hips. "I need you to spank *me*."

Finally, I've surprised him. I'll take that as two points, though I've long lost track of the score.

"But this time" —I draw his tie through my fingers, pulling when I get to the end— "you need to fulfill the promise of dipping into the cookie jar."

His eyes spark. Without looking away from me, he reaches over to the desk beside him and hits the intercom. "Claudette, please make sure I'm not disturbed for the next ten minutes."

"Yes, Mr. Sebastian," she says, and I almost get jealous thinking of how many times in a day she gets to say that. *Yes, Mr. Sebastian. Whatever you say, Mr. Sebastian.*

He replies with a thank you (which earns him extra credit in my book because hard-working employees should be treated with decency from their superiors), and clicks the intercom off.

"Ten minutes? You're awfully confident." Honestly, I could probably come in two.

Without warning, he spins the chair then lifts me onto his desk. His hands linger on my hips, burning into my skin through the material of my skirt. "How about a counter offer?"

He's not in a place to negotiate. I came in with the blackmail this time. I'm supposed to be the one in charge. He can't be proposing counter offers.

But I'm too curious not to hear him out. *Damn, him.* "Go on."

"How about we skip the spanking." He trails his palms down my thighs until they reach the end of my skirt. "And get right to the cookie jar."

He pushes my skirt up, and I'm not going to lie, the expression he makes when he sees what's there—or *isn't* there, more accurately—will forever be seared in my memory. It's the look that someone wears when they bite into something uniquely delicious. Like saffron crème brûlée or double nut baklava. I've seen the look many a time—worn it many more times.

I never thought someone would wear that look when they were looking at me.

"No panties?" His voice is scratchy. The same way I imagine his beard will feel between my thighs. "You walked out there in the world like this?"

Finally, he shows signs that he's human. I was beginning to think he only played for the sport and not the prize. "It was a well-kept secret, I assure you."

"Mm." He pushes his hands back up my thighs until his thumbs graze the edges of my pussy. "I think I forgot what I was saying."

"You were saying that you'd skip the spanking and go right to the cookies, which I'm fine with by the way." I spread my legs to give him better access to the jar.

"Ah, yes. My counter offer." He begins to massage my skin with the pads of his thumbs. Not quite where I'd like them to be massaging, but near enough to send all my blood to the area and fatten my clit into a hot, swollen nub. "No spanking, but you have to do something in exchange."

Of course there'd be a catch. "Do what?"

"You have to list ten reasons why you shouldn't go out with me before I make you come."

The caress of his thumbs is distracting, and I'm finding it hard to concentrate. But I'm pretty sure the only thing I liked in that sentence he just said was the part where he said he'd make me come. "Why on earth would I do that?"

"Because if you do, then we're even."

"And if I don't?"

"Then *you* owe *me*." He moves inward now, spreading my lips apart with his fingers then leans forward to blow softly against my sensitive skin.

It's maddeningly teasy, and I shudder with annoyed delight. I'm ready to get to the part where he makes me come and pronto. "Let me get this straight. I list ten reasons why I shouldn't go out with you before I come, and we're even. If I come before that, I owe you." Owe him a date, I'm guessing. The thought makes me all sorts of giddy, which I'd never admit because gross.

And I come either way.

Sort of sounds like I win no matter what.

"Are you in?" He sends another stream of air against my throbbing clit, and fuck, if he keeps this up, I'm going to come entirely too soon. I mean, the guy really deserves to work for it.

Obviously, I'm in.

Instead of answering, I start counting. "One, I'm out of your league."

He lowers his head, but not before I catch his grin.

Then he attacks the cookie jar in earnest, swirling his thumb over my clit with varying pressure that is sometimes just right but more often almost just right, and the man is an expert because that almost just right is really doing the job at getting me there in a hurry.

I force myself not to give into the pleasure. "Two. I only date men who respect women."

"You don't think I respect women?"

I level a glare. "You let me choke. Which is reason number three, by the way." The last words come out more of a jumble because he's suddenly added a finger to the action, tracing my entrance with the tip.

"You weren't choking."

"Four, you argue with everything I say."

"Then say things that don't deserve argument."

I screw my face up, as much from his statement as from the pleasure that feels awfully close to cresting. "What do I say that deserves argument? I'm smart, and I only speak to things I know something about. I'm brash, but I'm honest. I'm only combative when provoked."

Asshole has the nerve to laugh.

"What's funny?"

"Your warped sense of self." He inserts two fingers inside me, still teasing with the just right/almost just right pressure on my clit, and immediately finds the spot inside me that makes me bonkers.

Letting out a cry, I reach out a hand to his shoulder to steady myself.

"Also, you're about to come."

"Am not."

"And you claim to be honest. Liar."

"Six—"

"You skipped five."

"Five, you don't believe women." It's too much—the dance of his fingers inside and out, plus the unsatiated state that he left me in yesterday—I'm struggling not to Niagara Falls all over Steele's desk.

Honestly, I'm only punishing myself. That was likely his plan all along. Forcing me to think while he abuses my pussy—he knew it would stifle the pleasure. As soon as I surrender, I can truly enjoy what he's doing to me, and get to go on a date with him where he might even do this to me again.

It's a pride thing that makes me attempt to go further. I have to at least show a good fight before giving in. "Six—"

But then he leans his face in and swipes up my slit with his tongue. Liquid pools around his fingers. "Six?"

"Six, I hate people," I say in a rush. "And that includes you."

"You're definitely going to hate me now." He returns to my pussy, replacing the thumb on my clit with his hot mouth. His dirty, filthy mouth that, turns out, can do unspeakable things to a woman's peach. Licking, biting, sucking—all in deliberate rotation—and yes I hate him very much, and I proceed to tell him so until my body seizes and my pussy gushes and my eyes roll back into my head and pleasure lights my nervous system from head to toe like I'm goddamn Times Square.

Somewhere in the ecstasy of maybe the most amazing orgasm I've ever had, I have the cognizance to realize I'm really going to hate this prick if he ends up making me not hate him at all.

When I come to—I seriously might have blacked out for a second there—Steele is licking his finger clean like he's just had Kansas City barbeque.

So hot.

Steele, not the barbeque, though they do a nice job with the spice, I must say.

"You made a mess of my desk." He acts unaffected, but a glance at his bulging crotch says otherwise. "And you didn't finish the list."

"I didn't." I'm surprised how easily I admit it. Maybe it's because my defeat was too obvious or because of my post orgasmic haze. Or maybe just because it doesn't feel like a loss considering the terms. "Now I owe you."

"You do." He grabs a tissue from the box on his desk and cleans me up like a gentleman, causing me to rethink number two where I said he didn't respect women.

He finishes his cleaning with a kiss to my pubic bone. When he stands, he places another kiss on my nose, and my breath stutters. "Why do I like cleaning up after you so much, Simone Lima?"

I blush, but I play it off with a shrug. "Like I said. I'm out of your league. You'll do anything to be near me."

It's said in fun—we both know which of us is top shelf, and it's not the one of us who has been freshly fucked—but there's a part of me that wants to believe it. I think I even *could* believe it, if I'm not careful.

Not wanting to be *that* girl, the one who gets obsessed and gaga over one expertly given O, I pull my skirt down and hop off his desk. "I'll be on my way now."

I start past him, but he puts a hand on the desk, his arm blocking my path. "Not so fast."

"What?" I didn't forget that I owe him. Are you kidding me? I'm already planning how I'll do my hair and what outfit I'm going to wear and what pair of panties I won't be putting on underneath.

"You know what." He leans in front of me to grab a pen. He uncaps it with his mouth (why does that turn my insides to molten lava?), and grabs my hand. Such a simple gesture, but my heart skips a beat, and my silly little brain starts singing Here Comes the Bride like he's about to propose.

Propose, he does not. But he writes an address on the back of my hand like we're in seventh grade, and that's almost just as swoony. "Are we going steady now?"

He smiles around the cap still in his mouth and waits until he's put it back on the pen to speak. "My place. Be there tomorrow at nine sharp."

"Nine at night?" He's not even going to feed me dinner first? I mentally make that number seven on the list I didn't finish.

"Nine AM." He throws the pen on the desk and steps back to let me pass.

"Nine in the morning?" A day date. Well, well, well. "I'm supposed to be at work."

"Your boss still out?"

I shrug because yes, but I'm not easy.

Okay, I'm not *that* easy.

"Take another personal day. You can spend it hating me instead."

"Sure," I say. "Though I'll spend it hating you, whether I'm with you or at the office."

Fine, Steele was right—I'm definitely a liar.

Chapter Six

I've been to Donovan's place many times. And his parents as well. It's not my first time experiencing the world of the richy rich.

But the Sebastians are a whole other level of rich, and if I wasn't aware of it before I exited the elevator into Steele's spacious penthouse apartment overlooking Riverside Drive, I am now being educated. The floor beneath my feet is black marble, the ceiling is brass plated, and the single piece of furniture in the foyer is a walnut console with what appears to be a solid gold base.

Most notably, though, is that I'm greeted by a prim but gorgeous woman with her hair up in a black pantsuit. Another personal assistant? A butler? A house manager? What kinds of employees does a bachelor billionaire with no children need?

The woman introduces herself as Mindy then leads me to a living/dining/kitchen area with luxury appliances, sleek modern furnishings, and floor to ceiling windows. "Mr. Sebastian will be with you shortly," she says. "I'll be back in a moment with what you are to wear."

What I'm to wear?

Is Steele one of those bossy dominant types who controls the women he dates and tells them how to dress and who to talk to and when to come? I'm sure that's supposed to be a red flag, but the idea makes my thighs vibrate like a hummingbird.

The asshole better have good taste, and he better know I'm never leaving Donovan.

I decide I should let him know that sooner rather than later, and plot how I can introduce that to our relationship as I stare out at the greenery across the street.

"The view can be distracting."

I turn to find Steele dressed in designer slacks, sans tie and jacket, the top buttons of his crisp white shirt unbuttoned and the sleeves rolled up.

No man has a right to look that good disheveled. Talk about distracting. "I'm not quitting my job for you," I blurt out, before I can stop myself.

He only looks mildly thrown by the comment. "Right. You took a personal day."

"Yes. So, I'm not usually available on a Thursday morning like this."

"Okay." He waits a beat for me to—I don't know—clarify my earlier remark. When I don't, he goes on. "Anyway. Kitchen's here," he says, pointing out the obvious. "My study is down this hall on the right. Bathroom on the left. Mindy should be getting you your outfit."

I'm starting to have a feeling that I've missed something. "About that...Is what I'm wearing not appropriate?"

He scans my terracotta-colored puff sleeve dress—low cut and high leg, though not so short that my missing panties are an issue—then returns his gaze to mine. "I prefer my staff to wear less colorful outfits. Keeps things more orderly. Or did you mean just in general? In general, the dress is fine enough."

I've definitely missed something because:

1. This dress is premium date-wear. It's not, in any universe, just "fine enough".

2. "Keeps things more orderly" ...for whom? I'm sensing he was one of those boys in school who would blame a bad grade on the "distracting" spaghetti straps worn by the girl seated next to him. In which case, I'm about to puke.

3. Did he just refer to me as *staff*?

Much as I hate to admit I'm not anything but on the ball, I take a step toward him. "Um, just why exactly do you think I'm here?"

He points at me with a way-too-satisfied grin. "You're here because you lost."

"I lost, and that meant I owed you a..." I quickly play back the conversation from yesterday, and realize he never actually said this was a date. He had me list reasons I shouldn't date him, which led to my assumption that this was a date, but he never actually said that.

That whole stupid quip about assuming making you an ass never felt more accurate.

God, I'm stupid. But I think I can salvage this if I just don't let him know.

"Oh. Did you assume something else was going on here?"

…And he already knows.

Already knows because it was likely what he wanted me to assume. His triumphant expression makes me feral. That fucker is good, I'll give him that. And quick. Laying that trap on the fly.

Either I hate him more than anyone I've ever hated before, or I'm starting to fall for the guy. Hard to tell.

"Fine." It's as close as I'll get to admitting anything. "I'm here. What fucked up chore are you planning to dump on me?"

"Come on. What kind of a guy do you think I am?" The down and dirty type. That's what kind. "You're an experienced personal assistant, which is exactly what I intend to use you for since my usual personal assistant is out."

"Claudette?"

"Claudette's my PA at the office. Lola is my PA at home."

For fuck's sake. How many assistants does this guy have? "Mindy isn't your home PA?"

"She's my house manager. Totally separate tasks. Anyway, point being, Lola is out getting a boob job, so my home office has gotten out of hand. I thought you could help get it all cleaned up."

Any time a man shows respect for my organizational skills, they've won my devotion. Seriously, it's a wonder that I don't get on my knees right now. Though, with all the attractive women around, Steele might get that sort of appreciation on the regular.

I try to pretend that it doesn't make me jealous. "At least it's good to know you pay your employees enough to afford cosmetic work."

He laughs. "Lola's boob job? Don't be ridiculous. I'm paying for it."

Yeah, he definitely has an interesting relationship with his staff.

Before I can ask more questions that I probably don't want to know the answer to, Mindy arrives with my "outfit". She hands it over in a sealed plastic bag, and sure enough, it's black and boring. Probably another pantsuit. Hopefully, it fits. I'm an average weight, but five foot ten puts me on the tall side.

"Thank you, Mindy," Steele says before turning to me. "We'll be working in the office, if you want to change in the bathroom I mentioned earlier…"

"Yeah, yeah. I'll do that."

I venture down the hall and find the powder room just where he said it would be. Once the door's shut, I stare at myself in the mirror and try to properly assess the situation. Up until now, I thought we'd been playing some kinky filthy back and forth thing, but if Steele wants me to do some real work for him—well. I don't know how to feel about that.

On the one hand, I really do love a good organizational task.

On the other, I'd rather have my pussy licked.

I suppose the best of worlds would include both.

With a sigh, I open the package and shake out the outfit, and burst into laughter when I discover it's not a pantsuit at all, but a maid's uniform. The French maid type. Complete with a white apron. Short and sexy, and yeah. This is definitely still a kinky filthy game.

Does Mindy know?

Does he play this game with her as well? And Claudette? And Lola? It would explain why he's paying for her implants. He's probably the one who encouraged her to get them.

But seriously, what do I expect? He's a billionaire. He can mix business with pleasure all he wants. It's not like I'm looking for anything but fun myself, so do I really care what he's doing with his employees?

If I do care, I'll never admit it. Not even to myself.

And that means that a few minutes later, I'm dressed in the outfit and ready to "work". With no panties, my ass cheeks are on display, so I scurry out of the bathroom and to the office before Mindy sees me. Even if she's aware of what I'm really here for, I prefer my sexcapades happen in private.

I find Steele seated, not behind his desk, but in an armchair with a digital tablet in hand. He doesn't look up when I enter.

I pull the door shut behind me and pose myself in a sexy-lean-against-the-wall pose.

"Keep it open, please." He still doesn't look at me.

"I'm sorry, but I don't feel comfortable leaving the door open when I'm dressed like this."

"Lola doesn't mind."

"Lola wears this same outfit?"

Finally, he looks up, and stoic as he's pretending to be, he can't hide his hooded gaze. "Not exactly that outfit, I suppose. Longer, maybe. The service has their own uniforms, and I don't usually pay attention."

Then maybe he isn't fucking Lola, but now I'm getting a different interpretation of what's going on here. "Wait a minute…is Lola your housekeeper?"

"Housekeeper. Personal assistant. Same thing, right? I know some of you are sensitive about the actual label."

Rage boils through my body. "You think the job I do is equivalent to a housekeeper?" Not to knock housekeepers. They deserve the utmost respect, and if it were my job, I would hate it when anyone conflated that work with something that it wasn't, and I would hate it as much as I am right now. "I am not a goddamned housekeeper, Steele. I'm an exceptionally skilled personal *office* assistant."

"And we're in an office. So…" He waggles his fingers like he's shooing me to work. "The bookcases are gathering a layer of dust. And don't forget the trash bin."

He goes back to his tablet, swiping his screen as though he's reading a book.

Reading a book while he expects me to clean his motherfucking office.

I'm seventy-five percent sure that the asshole has to be pulling my leg. *Has to be.* Right? But the twenty-five percent part of me that's uncertain is mad enough to take over my whole personality. He wants me to dust his office? He wants me to empty his trash?

Fine.

On *my* terms.

I scan the room and find a decorative doily under one of his plants. (Admittedly, the fact that he has real live plants in his bachelor pad, makes me hate him a smidge less.) I move the plant off the ornamental lace, and study it long enough to realize it's delicate, most likely antique, and definitely not something that should be used for cleaning tasks, but Steele should have thought of that before he put me to work for the day.

Ignoring the bookshelves closest to me, I cross to the ones right behind him and start my dusting there. One shelf in, and the doily is already filthy. It's as if the shelves haven't been cleaned in weeks. I'm pretty sure a boob job doesn't take a woman out for more than a couple. Either Lola has been gone longer, or she's not a very good housekeeper.

As tempting as it is to prove I can do a better job, that's not my goal right now. With the first shelf done, I bend to clean the one below it, and do I stick my naked butt in Steele's face when I bend?

You bet my sweet ass I do.

I stick it in his face, and wiggle it around. Bent over like this, he has a view of my pussy as well. I wait a beat for him to make a move.

Then another beat.

Finally, I peer over my shoulder to see what he's doing, and the fucker isn't even looking. Frustration doesn't begin to describe how I'm feeling, until I notice that there is a very definitive bulge in that billionaire's lap.

Pretending he didn't peek when obviously he did.

Or maybe he just gets off on the whole scenario in general.

Either way, he's on my hook, whether he likes it or not, which means I need to deliver more of the same. This time, I attack the higher shelves. I get all of the ones I can reach easily, then kick off my Prada black pumps.

Then, with the doily in hand, I grab onto Steele's shoulder and start to hoist myself onto the arm of his chair.

"What the hell are you doing?" Despite his irritation, his hand wraps around my calves, steadying me.

"I can't reach," I explain, as if he's an idiot. When I let go of his shoulder, there's dirt on his white shirt, and I have to literally bite my lip to keep from smiling as I stretch to reach the higher shelves.

He continues to hold my legs as I dust, the warmth of his fingers sending a jolt through my nervous system.

I'm not the only one affected.

When I glance down, his bulge has grown, and Steele isn't even trying to hide that his eyes are focused like a laser up my skirt.

I'm pleased, but I'm not done.

After finishing another shelf, I pull my foot out of his grasp and place it on his (dirty) shoulder, so I can reach the highest shelf.

Or so I can pretend I'm reaching for the highest shelf.

Really it just spreads my legs so he can have a better view. And when he's fully distracted, I put weight on that foot—weight he isn't prepared to take—and surprise, surprise, I topple into his lap.

If I wasn't sure he was hard before, I'm definitely sure now. It's jabbing into my lower back like it's a gun at a stick-up, and I'm more than ready to be robbed.

"Whoops." I throw my arms around his neck and smile innocently.

"What do you think you're doing?" Steele's voice is a rasp as his hands settle on me. Not-so-innocently settle, I might add. One grazing the side of my breast, the other wrapped around the curve of my bare ass.

"What do you think *you're* doing?"

"You're in my lap."

"You're fondling my ass."

It might be my imagination, but his mouth seems to move an inch closer to mine. "It's a very nice ass."

"It's a very nice lap." I wiggle my butt and grin when his cock twitches. "I'm starting to have a feeling this is where you wanted me all along. Was that your plan?"

He shakes his head, but his eyes disagree, and his mouth closes in more. "I don't think I'm capable of planning where you're concerned. You make me crazy, and I just react, and next thing you know, I'm canceling my schedule so I can work from home and ordering a sexy maid costume to arrive overnight."

My grin widens. "That does sound crazy."

His lips brush mine. "You're a dirty distraction in my life that I do not need."

"Sounds like a personal problem." This time when his lips brush mine, I tilt my neck so my mouth meets his.

That's all the invitation he needs.

The hand on my ass comes up to hold my chin in place and then he kisses me like he's been dying to kiss me since we've met. Like he's only been barely holding back. Like he might never stop kissing me.

Ten seconds in, and I've already ranked it on my top five kisses of all time.

There's a very good chance it could end up ranked higher, except just as it's really starting to get good, Steele stands up with me in his arms.

Yes! Show me your bedroom please, sir.

Instead, he sets me on my feet and bends me over his desk.

"Fuck, Simone. The dirty, filthy things I want to do to you…"

"Whatever those things are, please tell me they include putting your cock so far inside me I feel it for days."

He moans. "I'm adding that to the list."

"There's a list?" I didn't think I could be any wetter.

"You better believe there's a list." He flips my skirt up and slaps one ass cheek. "That's for being so goddamned sexy I can't think straight." He slaps the other cheek. "That's because you love that you do that to me."

"How do you know me so well?" I'm not sure if I should be

frightened or planning our China patterns.

Let's be honest, though—I plan China patterns just for fun.

"Because you speak to my soul." He drops to his knees and laps my pussy from behind. "I've been craving this taste for the last twenty four hours. It was driving me insane."

I will never belittle the madness of a deep craving, but I'm dealing with a madness of my own. "Back to that list...how long before your dick makes an appearance?"

He laps the length of my slit all the way to my asshole, and I suddenly have no idea why I'm complaining because this is working out for me just fine.

"I want to hear your list, baby."

I have always detested generic endearments, so obviously I have to hate myself now because his use of *baby* makes my legs jelly.

His tongue on my cunt might also contribute to the weakness.

"How about you tell me seven ways you want me to fuck you before the day is over, and I'll let you come?" He sticks his tongue inside me, and I'm so out of my mind, I almost agree.

"No, I don't trust you."

"You don't trust I'll make you come?"

"I don't trust I'll get your cock. And I really, really want your cock."

He practically growls, the sound vibrating across my sensitive bits, and all my blood rushes to my clit. "I promise, I'll give you my cock. But first, seven ways you want me to fuck you." He returns to his assault.

"Um, okay. Standing up."

"More specific."

I groan at the interruption of his tongue. Then melt when it returns. Desperate to not have to endure its absence again, I quickly imagine a scenario, and hope it's what he wants. "Me on this desk, you standing, my legs wrapped around your waist."

"One," he says, and I celebrate internally when he barely breaks to say the word.

Okay, okay. I got this.

"In your bed, with you hovering above my face while I suck you off. That's two."

I swear he starts tracing the number two against my clit.

"In the main room, me naked against your windows while you choke me from behind. That's three."

Oh yeah, that one's good. God, I might come sooner than number seven.

"Don't you dare come before the list is done."

It's like he can read my thoughts.

And his mouth is gone again, but I'm not too mad because he stands, and I hear the sound of his zipper. "Keep going, Simone."

"Four, on the sofa, me riding your lap. My tits bouncing."

"My palms squeezing them tight." He reaches around me to palm one of my breasts through my dress, a demonstration of sorts.

"Yes. Harder. Tweak my nipple."

He doesn't do as I ask, because he's a fucker, but even better, a hard, velvet ridge slides across my soaked pussy.

I start to turn to try to get a glance at the glorious cock rubbing against my goodies, but he pushes me back down. "The list. Number five."

He sounds as eager as I feel. "Number five—on your kitchen table. Reverse cowgirl. While I fondle your balls."

The sound he makes as he smacks my pussy with his cock almost undoes me. "Two more, and I'll get a condom."

"Against the wall, one of my legs stretched up on your shoulder."

"Are you that flexible?"

"Don't you want to find out?"

He circles my rim with his tip. "You are—"

But I don't get to hear the end of that sentiment because voices drift in from outside the office door (the one I never opened when told).

"He's in his office, but he's busy at the moment," Mindy says.

"I don't care if he's busy. He's on my clock right now."

I've only heard it a few times, but Steele's brother has a distinct voice that I would recognize anywhere.

"Fuck." Steele backs up. I turn to see him quickly tucking himself away. "Fuck. You have to hide," he says, buckling his belt.

I'm not keen on being caught in this outfit myself, especially not with my cunt crying all over the place, but as far as I can see there are no closets so I'm not sure where to go.

Steele is quicker than I am. "Under there." He pulls me with him toward his desk pushing me to my knees just as Holt bursts through the door.

Quickly, I crawl underneath. Steele drops into his chair and rolls closer, practically sealing off my hiding place. "Jesus, don't you knock?"

I feel the tension.

Of course I do.

But really, we're only in this position because of Steele and his antics.

And sure, he's a great kisser, and solid gold with good tongue, but he's also conniving, and truth is, he makes me crazy too. Besides, he promised me his cock.

So even though this might be the worst idea ever, the thing I'm about to do next?

Totally his own fault.

Chapter Seven

I'm one of those women who loves giving blow jobs for several reasons:

1. It allows me to stay impersonal
2. It gives me control
3. I have an oral fixation and love putting lots of different things in my mouth
4. I'm amazing at them

Honestly, this is a gift. Steele owes me right now, as far as I'm concerned, because not only did he promise me his cock, I did dust, like, seven of his shelves. Seven out of seventy might be a low percentage of work completion, but I would have done more if his brother hadn't shown up. Probably.

In other words, I have no guilt as I slide my hand up the inside of Steele's thigh toward the bulge straining against his fly.

"Is there a reason you're barging into my study?" To his credit, he doesn't sound like a man who is about to be assaulted under his desk.

"It seems like the only way to get a hold of you these days since you aren't at the office and you aren't answering my calls."

I cup Steele's cock through his trousers, giving it a little squeeze. As though I've just knocked on the door, he widens his legs, letting me in. "Well, you're here. What now?"

He's talking to Holt, but I think he's also talking to me. Daring me. Does he think I won't?

I start to work on carefully undoing his belt, proving that I most definitely will.

"I have a meeting down the street in an hour. Thought I'd stop by to take another stab at convincing you to—"

Steele cuts him off. "Could we talk about it later? I'm in the middle of—"

I'm intrigued to hear what he's going to say he's in the middle of, but Holt interrupts. "You can sure tell Lola hasn't been here. These shelves have an inch of dust. You haven't brought in a replacement while she's gone?"

"I have, actually. Guess she's not that good."

Belt and button undone, I pause before moving on to his zipper so that I can flick my finger against the spot where I think his crown is.

He jolts.

"You okay?" Holt asks.

Steele reaches under the desk and flicks the side of my forehead. "Just an itch. What's going on with Hunter?"

I'm not interested in whoever this Hunter character is, and I tune out the conversation and concentrate on quietly unzipping his fly. Once down, I reach my hand down the pouch of his boxer briefs and work his cock free.

Work is probably the wrong word because it doesn't take much at all to get the beast free.

And beast is definitely the right word because, as I'd suspected, Steele Sebastian is hung and standing proud.

You should *stand proud, my boy. You deserve to boast.*

I fondle the beast to get my bearings, running both my hands down his length then cup his balls before trailing my fingers back up his shaft. Then I swipe a palm over his head, and practically moan. He's soft and velvety and thick and strong—everything I love in a cock.

On cue, a bead of pre-cum sprouts at the tip, and I bend forward to lap it up, making my tongue flat as it sweeps across his crown.

Meanwhile, I'm half aware of Holt's voice in the background, seemingly moving across the room, so I notice the abrupt tone change. "What the fuck, Steele? You, uh, playing hanky panky with Mindy now?"

A strange jealousy that I have no right to possess bubbles inside me, and I hate how curious I am to hear more. Hate wanting to know what inspired the comment in the first place. Hate it so much that I take my aggression out on Steele, drawing my teeth lightly across his tip.

"They're not Mindy's shoes," he says through gritted teeth. *My pumps!* I'd forgotten about them. "Had someone over earlier."

Clever because it's not a lie.

I apologize for my assumption with another sweep of my tongue.

"And she left without her shoes?" Steele must make some sort of contrary expression in response. "Oh, she's still here?"

This time I peer up to see Steele give an elusive shrug.

"Mm. No wonder you wanted to work from home." They share a laugh, and I'm not sure if Holt presumes that Steele has a girl waiting in his bedroom or if he suspects that I'm actually under the desk.

Whichever it is, he seems to not care to know more and goes back to discussing "Hunter" and "the board" and "Dad" and a shit load of other boring things that sound work and family related.

And that means I'm done listening in.

With Lil Wayne playing in my head, I get to licking Steele's lollipop, lapping my tongue up the side of his shaft, using lots of saliva, then sucking his crown lightly before repeating the process. I do it again and again, enjoying the tensing of his thighs as I tease him, knowing that what I'm doing feels good but isn't quite what he wants.

The more I play, the more he stirs, shifting in his seat. He drops his hands to his thighs. He clears his throat. Coughs once. Spreads his legs wider. Little by little, I notice the conversation becomes more one-sided. The gap between Holt's words and Steele's responses grows. He sinks down in his chair, pushing his cock in my face, a not so subtle hint to get it on, and if that's really what he wants…

I wait until he's mid-sentence— "Hunter doesn't really want your job. He wants—" And that's when I take him down my throat.

All the way.

And I mean *all the way*, so that every last inch of him is in my mouth.

I feel his thighs shiver as they frame my face, and his breathing stutters.

"He wants…what?" Holt prods.

"I, uh." He clears his throat again. "I lost my train of thought. Sorry."

I smirk as I pull my lips back across his length, only to deep-throat him once again. Again and again, speeding up each bob of my head. When I glance up at him, his eyes are hooded. He takes a long blink then swallows.

The guy is not going to last long. I can't decide if it's more torturous to leave him this aroused or to let him try and hide an epic orgasm.

I'm still deciding—still torturing—when Holt uses Steele's lost thought to turn the conversation. "Anyway. About the Kincaid story— I'm stalled out on my end. Can you—?"

"I don't want to talk about this right now," Steele says, seeming to know what Holt is going to say. Seeming to not want me to hear him say it.

But he's talking about my boss, and now I'm hyper focused on the conversation. I pull back, about to let his cock fall out of my mouth, when Steele's hands clasp around my ears. Holding me in place, he thrusts in, surprising me with the force and tempo.

Okay, number one—hot.

Number two? If he thinks I can't listen and/or concentrate while I'm being face-fucked, he's wrong.

"Does that mean you haven't made a move on his secretary yet? I think if you just get close to her—"

Three things happen all at once:

1. Steele freezes with his cock shoved down my throat.

2. I start to choke.

3. Holt's phone rings.

"I've got to take this," Holt says. "Yes? I'm...sure. Okay." The next comment sounds like it's directed to his brother. "I have to deal with this. I'll call you later. Answer this time." Then, "I'm actually on my way to meet with them right now."

His voice fades, and I'm pretty sure he's left the room.

Meanwhile, I'm still choking.

I ball my fists and beat on Steele's thighs. A few seconds of this, and he finally lets go of my head. "Okay. He's gone."

I shove him so his chair moves back and climb out from under the desk. "What the goddamned fuck was that?"

He smiles like this is all still fun and games. "You were choking."

So now *he admits I was choking.* "I was not choking."

Before I can go on, he jumps in. "You were most definitely choking. I know choking when I see it. Couldn't handle what I have to offer?"

"I wasn't choking, you asshole. I was being choked." There's a difference, and if he doesn't know what it is, I'm not in the mood to explain it right now. "What was your brother talking about?"

At least he has the good sense to look guilty. "I know. You're not a secretary. Holt isn't always considerate about labels, but I know they matter."

The fucker really knows how to woo me.

Or rather, *try* to woo me because it's not going to work. I will not be distracted from his deceit with his charm.

"I am not an idiot, Steele." I stomp over to the chair to retrieve my pumps. "I heard what he said. I get the implication. I know this thing with me was all about getting to Donovan."

"It's not like it sounds. I never—"

"I'm not an idiot," I say again, pointing a narrow heel in his direction.

"I never took you for an idiot, Simone." He stands, tucking away his magnificent (and still erect) cock, seeming to understand (correctly) that I'm not finishing him off now. "And yes, my brother asked me to get close to you, but I never agreed to do it."

"Yeah, it sure looks like you never agreed to do it." I stomp to the door, peering down the hall to make sure Holt really is gone and Mindy isn't in sight before rushing to the bathroom.

Steele is right on my heels, but I manage to slam the door in his face. "None of this is about Holt," he says through the wood barrier.

"Of course not. You just randomly show up at women's offices and demand to spank them." I practically rip the French maid's outfit off of my body then panic momentarily because I didn't look to see if my dress was still there waiting for me.

Fortunately, it is.

"It wasn't random. It was a natural follow up to what we'd started the day before."

"Yeah, sure. Sure."

"If it wasn't, then why did you show up at my office the day after that? We have a connection, and you know it."

Well, I *thought* we'd had a connection.

Oh, fuck. Was Donovan the reason why he sat by me at the dinner in the first place? Was this all a ruse from the start?

He really must think I'm stupid.

And maybe I am because all of this should have seemed fucked up to me before now. There were plenty of red flags. I mean, I have no issues with confidence, but he's a billionaire. I'm a secretary. (Not really a secretary, but as far as his type is concerned, I am.) We don't run in the same circles. We don't exist in the same world.

Dressed, I swing open the door and almost laugh when he stumbles back. "Serves you right."

I start down the hall toward the door.

"Think about it, Simone." He's right behind me as I go. "Have I asked you anything about Kincaid in our time together? How does a spanking get you to spill information about your boss? Why would I need you to hide today if I was doing what Holt asked me to do?"

I slow my pace. I'm not ready to give him the benefit of the doubt, but he asks some good questions, and except when I think I'm being asked out on a day date by a dirty, hot rich man, I try not to make assumptions without more knowledge.

"That kiss, Simone," he says, knowing he has my attention. "There is no way you can deny that kiss was real."

I turn to him, arms crossed over my chest protectively. "I don't know anything about you, Steele."

"That's not true. You know how good it feels to have my hands on you, you know how my cock feels down your throat, and you know you want to keep exploring whatever this is between us." Before I can deny it, he adds, "Don't lie to me. Be honest."

"Honest." I huff. "I can't trust you. Why would I be honest?"

"Because I'm being honest. I don't want this to end before it has a chance to get good. And, Simone? I think it could be real good."

And this is why I hate people—because it takes so much work to build trust, and yet if you want any sort of relationship, you have to trust even to begin. It's a lot of energy. Too many times I've put too much of myself out there too early and been hurt.

Have I done that again with Steele?

So far it's just been body parts and saliva. My heart is still safe behind its cage.

He hasn't moved, but it feels like he's closing in on me. I take a step backward. "I don't even know what this is, Steele. This isn't how people do something real. You know, they go on a date. He shares his boring biography. She laughs at his lame jokes. He pays way too much for a mediocre dinner. She pretends she's not going to let him fuck her, but she shaved everything earlier, so of course she is."

He wrinkles up his nose. "Sounds kind of boring."

Yeah, it usually kind of is.

But it's a formula I know. A formula I have faith in. Whatever this is with Steele, it's too new. Too undefined. Too much of a risk.

The elevator opens as soon as I push the button. I step in and turn to him. "I don't know what your intentions were with me, Mr. Sebastian, but I think this game has run its course."

"Simone—"

I hit the door closed button, and the rest of his sentence is lost as I drop down.

Chapter Eight

When I come into work the next morning—early, because I'm devoted to my job, and I like to get started before the whole place is brimming with people—Donovan's walking out of his office.

He's dressed in khakis and a Henley instead of his usual suit, but he's still intimidating when he glares at me. "What are you doing here?"

"What are *you* doing here?"

"I'm headed up to the Hamptons with Sabrina for the weekend, maybe longer. I had some files at home I wanted to drop off." He nods to my desk where he's stacked a bunch of manilla folders. He was also in his office, though, so I suspect there's something else he needed that he doesn't want to share.

That's Donovan for you. Secrets and secrets and more secrets.

I flip through the labels on the files. We're mainly digital these days, and whatever is here will probably need to be uploaded. It gives me something to do with the day, at least. "I'll get working on these."

"Now you."

I raise a brow.

"I thought you were taking personal days."

Oh. Yeah. Back when I'd hoped that yesterday's day date would turn into two. "Just one personal day." I sit down behind my desk, throw my purse in the bottom drawer, and lock it. "Back to the grind today. My boss is a tyrant. Don't want to get behind."

"Complete tyrant." He nods to his office door. "I'll leave this open?"

"I'll lock it up." I wiggle my mouse to boot up the computer as he passes to leave and start making a mental list of tasks for the day.

1. Upload files
2. Don't think about Steele
3. Reschedule Monday's meetings
4. Don't think about Steele
5. Lock up Donovan's office
6. Don't think about Steele
7. Don't think about Steele
8. Don't think about Steele

"What's wrong?"

I look up to realize Donovan is still here, watching me with narrow eyes. "Nothing's wrong."

"Don't bullshit me. What's wrong?"

That's the other thing about Donovan. He always knows. Everything. Seriously, everything. I'm sure he even knows I steal his invites, has probably known since day one, but the advantage of working with a secret-keeper is that he lets me keep my secrets too.

Usually.

Apparently, not today.

Just because he's trying to nose me out, doesn't mean I have to open up. He has enough on his plate with his family emergency. "Oh, nothing new. I just hate everyone."

He nods like he understands, and for half a second, I think he's going to let that be the end of it.

But I'm wrong. "Is this about that Sebastian guy?"

"What? Who? Holt?" I'm not good at playing dumb. I just don't want to talk about it, and I hope he takes the cue.

He levels his stare. "You know who I mean. Why don't you want to talk about it?"

Told you he knows everything.

Fine then. I spin my chair in his direction to give him my full attention. "What's up with you and his brother?"

"Holt?" Donovan isn't the best at playing dumb either. But he's very good at not saying what he doesn't want to say, and I'm sure that's where he's headed now. "He wanted information from me that I didn't want to give."

"Oh." I'm so surprised he answered, that's all I have to say.

"I thought that your Steele character might be using you to get to me."

I force a laugh, pretending I don't have a pit in my stomach. I don't want to think about this. Don't want to hear my fears validated by a man I respect, so I turn my focus back to my computer screen. "That's absurd. You don't tell me anything."

"Right. Absurd."

"And he's not *my* Steele."

"Of course not. Because you hate everyone."

"Exactly." I start to key in my login and pause to glance up at my boss. "What did he say to you?"

"Steele? Yeah, that's the thing." He crosses over to my side of the desk and I tense as he sits/leans on the edge, invading my space. "He didn't seem to have any idea what I was talking about when I accused him of using you to get info for his brother."

"He didn't?" I fucking hate how hopeful I sound. It's embarrassing. "And you believe him?"

"Yeah, I think I do. Seemed much more interested in you owing him or something like that." He stands now, his height towering above me. "Now if you've gotten yourself into some shit with this guy, and you need help getting out of it…"

Daddy Donovan out to fight the mighty Sebastians on my behalf.

I bite back a smile. "No. He's…" *Harmless*, I suppose.

Except not at all harmless because whether or not he was spying for his brother, he has the power to make me feel like this—whatever this mood that I don't want to examine too closely is—and that feels exactly the opposite of harmless. "It doesn't matter anymore. I hate everyone."

"Right, right."

The lights down the hall flicker on. Nate's assistant must be in. A too-cheery woman who turns on lights and opens blinds and hums wherever she goes.

I scowl. My chance for pre-workday alone time is gone.

"Anyway." Donovan steps back to the other side of my desk (the side he belongs on). "Sabrina's waiting for me."

"Bye." I go back to the mental task list:

1. It doesn't matter about Steele

2. Don't think about Steele

"The thing about saying you hate everyone, Simone…"

I throw my head back. "For fuck's sake, are you going to actually leave?" Before he can continue on like I haven't interrupted, I stare him down. "Please don't tell me you're going to lecture me on relationships. You might be happily married, but you know as well as I do, that you have never been a role model in human interaction."

"No. Definitely not a role model. Doesn't mean I don't know a thing or two about psychology."

"So, let me guess—you're going to tell me that I don't really hate everybody, right? That that's just something I say so I don't have to put myself out there. So I don't have to trust new people. And that this whole overly confident, detached persona of mine is just a ruse and really I'm soft and squishy and gross inside, with a fragile heart that I keep hidden so that it won't get broken. Something like that?"

"You said it. Not me." He smirks—he's famous for his smirk. "I was just going to say that I hoped 'everyone' didn't include me."

I glare. "You're the top of the list, Kincaid. Top of the list."

He winks, and I still hate him. A little bit less, but still more than anyone else. "Hey, when you chill out in my office later to watch your soaps and, uh, whatever else you do in there—make sure you clean up after yourself this time, will you?"

My face goes red.

He really does know *everything.*

"It's daytime television," I yell after him since he's (finally) leaving. "Not soaps." I shudder at the thought.

Then blush again, wondering exactly what else he knows happened in that office, and ultimately resolve to put it out of my mind and never think about it again.

And then I start the day's tasks. I upload the physical files and consider calling Steele.

Then I file the physical files and remember I don't have his direct line.

Then I reschedule half of Monday's meetings and wonder if I should just call Claudette.

Then I reschedule the next half of Monday's meetings and decide I wouldn't know what to say.

Then I go into Donovan's office and dust his shelves (I've come to the conclusion that I'm quite good at this, *fuck you very much, Holt Sebastian*), and do a lot of sighing because even if I really am squishy on the insides, I don't know how to live without my shell, and how can I expect that anyone—particularly, anyone like Steele—could find their way past the hard exterior and want to stay?

I don't come to an answer, but it turns out *the answer* comes to *me*.

When I step out of Donovan's office, I find an extremely hot and arrogant billionaire holding red roses and waiting for me.

Chapter Nine

"What are you doing here?" The roses make it sort of obvious, but I'm prickly by nature, and that's what comes out.

Steele, I'm discovering, is able to meet me prick by prick. "What do you think I'm doing here?"

Several salty retorts cross my mind over a handful of seconds. I muster up the strength to swallow them all. "I don't think you were getting close to me for your brother."

"I know. I don't think I would have shown up here if I thought you really did."

Okay, that out of the way...

I cross the few steps between us and examine the roses in his hand. "They don't have thorns."

"I was afraid you'd cut yourself."

"You'd let a woman choke but not bleed. Progress, I suppose."

I take the vase from his hand, but before I can move to take them to my desk, he catches my waist and pulls me to him. His mouth hovers at my ear, hot and inviting. "I wouldn't let *you* bleed. I wouldn't let you choke either, if you were really choking, unless I'm choking you on purpose."

It's disgusting how fast my panties are ruined.

It's not just my libido that Steele affects. My chest feels tight and agitated, and I can't decide if I'm excited or terrified.

Both, perhaps.

"What are you doing here?" I can't face him, and this time when I ask, it's barely a whisper.

He leans his forehead against my scalp, and I can still feel each of his breaths as they skate across my lobe. "I came to ask you on a date."

My heart flutters. "You could have called."

"I didn't trust you to answer."

Dammit, he's too tuned into me. But I'm not entirely sure I mind. "I would have thought about answering."

"Progress, I suppose."

I can't help myself, I swivel my head to catch his grin. How can a man be so smug and sexy at the same time? Why am I so here for it? "A real date? No strings attached?"

"A real date. No strings attached."

I bite my lip so that I don't answer too quickly. "Okay. I'd like that."

As soon as I give him the yes, the man is in motion. He steps away from me and claps his hands together. "Mindy. Titus."

Mindy appears rolling a table with a cream tablecloth and stainless steel covered plates. A man follows—Titus, I presume—carrying two chairs.

"In there," Steele says, directing them to set-up in Donovan's office.

"Wait—what?" I chase after him as he follows the servers. "What is this?"

He ignores me. "It should be good right there. Thank you, Mindy. Titus, could you just push the couch a little to make room. Perfect. That's all."

"You can't! Oh my God. This isn't!" I'm so flustered, I can't finish a single thought. "Steele!"

His employees leave as quickly as they came, and finally he gives me his attention. "Yes, my love?"

The floor practically disappears from beneath me at the endearment, but I refuse to be caught swooning. "What on earth is this?"

"Lunch. Typically served midday, though the menu has more of a dinner feel. A compromise, since the ideal, of course, would be to actually share a meal at the time that dinner is usually served, but..."

He trails off, leaving me to fill in the rest. "You were afraid I wouldn't show."

"Bingo." He points a finger as he says the word. "And I owed you a day date."

This certainly isn't my definition of either "a real date" or "no-strings," but before I can get myself thoroughly worked up about it, I take a breath.

Then I laugh.

Because it turns out I'm not upset about it at all. It's actually very charming, and I'm entirely turned on about it.

Barely into the laugh, I bring my hand to cover my mouth. He doesn't get to win that easily. He still has to get through the date before I've made up my mind about him. Isn't that how it usually works? "All right then. A day date. In my boss's office."

He glances over at the floor to ceiling windows. "You normally have to pay top dollar for a restaurant view like that."

"Ah, so you didn't want to fork out the money."

He gives me a wry look. "I may have gone cheap on location, but I think you'll find the menu compensates. Sorry, not sorry, I couldn't bring myself to pay for a mediocre meal." He lifts a silver lid off a small dish and exposes a pear and pomegranate salad. When he removes a larger lid, he reveals steak tartare.

It's Monday night's menu. The meal I missed.

I can't help myself and clap my hands together in glee. "Saffron crème brûlée for dessert?"

"Saffron crème brûlée for dessert." He shrugs. "Or we can start with that, if you prefer."

"No, no. The traditional order of things is good."

He catches my gaze and holds it for a beat. I feel his stare everywhere—in my pinky toes and the back of my neck and the base of my spine and the corners of my lips. Seriously, if I keep grinning like this, my face is going to start to hurt.

If he keeps staring at me like this, lunch isn't going to happen at all.

As if he realizes the same thing, he drops his eyes and pulls out one of the chairs. "If you'd take a seat, please?"

I sit, and he drapes a napkin over my lap. Then he bends to look under the tablecloth, and I wonder if it won't be a traditional date after all. Which is disappointing, but I spread my legs anyway, not wanting to miss out if he's going for my pussy.

Apparently, there's storage underneath, and he's only going for an ice-bucket with champagne and two glasses. "I have sparkling cider as well."

My expression likely says how appalled I am at that suggestion.

"You are supposed to be working." But he pops open the bottle before I can tell him not to judge. "Also, I'm lying. There's no sparkling cider. I just wanted to appear thoughtful."

"Suggestion for the future—it works better if you don't admit it seconds after the fact."

He pours a glass and hands it to me. "Yes, in the future, I'll definitely see my lies through to the end, but I'm trying to deliver an experience here, and though you didn't mention 'no lying' in your description of a normal date, I suspect it was inferred."

I'm beginning to think the guy might be as unused to ordinary dating as I am.

It's possible we're made for each other.

The thought makes me shudder except it's more like a shiver and my chest feels all sorts of warm. I cover my reaction with a sip of champagne while Steele sits himself in the seat across from me. When he uncovers his salad, I pick up my fork and bite into mine.

God, it's fantastic.

Better than the salad from the other night, since it has real goat cheese instead of feta. I'm practically having a mouth orgasm, when Steele clears his throat.

"I'm thirty-four and the middle child of three."

"Okay." It's so out of nowhere, I don't know what else to say.

"Unless you count my secret half-brother, but I don't usually bring him up on a first date, so we'll leave that for later."

I swear I usually have no problem getting substances past my lips and down the right tube, and yet I nearly choke on a pomegranate seed.

"Are you—?"

I put my hand up and shake my head. A sip of champagne helps. "Nope. Just fine." My voice sounds raw, so I clear my throat. "Secret brother that we aren't going to talk about. Got it."

"My grandfather built a huge company focused on industrial materials and also, as a side hustle, started a news network." It's strange to hear Irving Sebastian, a man as famous as Rockefeller, reduced to a single sentence, and it's only at the arrival of this thought that I realize Steele is giving me his bio, a component of a "real date", according to my outburst yesterday at his apartment.

"My father took over as CEO when he was in his forties, and ran it until he had to step down for health reasons. My brother took his place after that. I work in the business and talent department because that's where Dad said I'd work, and pretty much everyone does what Dad says, for some reason."

"Maybe because he's one of the most powerful men in America?"

"I think his reach extends internationally."

"There you go."

"He's a hard, temperamental sort of man. Not at all loving, and since my mother died when I was five, we were taught to be equally as focused if we wanted any sort of attention from him. Or at least pretend to be as focused. Now, before you go feeling sorry for me, I must add that my Grandpa Irving is much less of an asshole and showers all of his grandkids with affection. Tough guy brand, but it counts. Oh, and I have a hundred million dollar trust fund, so I can more than make up for my lack of parental support and emotional development with therapy, good drugs, and nice cars."

"Well, then."

"You're supposed to laugh at my lame jokes." Another "real date" criteria.

"They can't be so lame I don't realize it's a joke."

He narrows his eyes. "Fine. Challenge accepted."

Over the next several minutes, Steele gives me more of his bio, sharing mundane resumé type details about where he went to school (Dalton for high school, Columbia for his bachelor, Yale for his masters) and what sports he played (crew and diving). Then he moved to the more interesting details of when he had his first kiss (with Missy Benson at age seven), when he had his first real kiss (with Sara Epstein at age thirteen), when he first had sex (Sara Epstein's stepmom at age fifteen), and when he last had a girlfriend (five years ago, it lasted three years, and he broke it off because he didn't enjoy the traditional structure of the relationship).

He manages to insert at least three identifiable lame jokes that I laugh at on cue. But he speaks in monologue, giving me very little chance to comment, which isn't really what I'd pictured when I'd given him my description of a "real date".

But I also realize that nothing he's told me is really useful knowledge. I mean, I know things about him now that I didn't before, but none of it gives me insight into how compatible we are or whether I want to spend more time with him or if we might share the same biting outlook on life.

I learned pretty much all the good stuff when he showed up wanting to spank me.

When I've long since cleared my salad plate (his remains untouched), he finally says, "I think that's all the important stuff. Anything I'm missing?"

I shake my head. Honestly, the only other thing I want to know right now is how good his cock feels inside me. The sooner we can get to that, the better. "Am I supposed to give you my bio now?"

He makes a face that says he finds the idea as unappealing as I do. "Unless you'd like to, but you didn't list reciprocation as a 'real date' requirement."

I run through my head to see where we are on that list:

1. His boring bio
2. Her laughs at his lame jokes
3. An expensive mediocre dinner
4. She pretends she isn't going to fuck him, but she shaved

As it just so happens, I shaved yesterday before going to his apartment.

In other words, the date's technically concluded.

And now I'm thinking about another list. All the places I wanted him to fuck me before the day was done.

I set my napkin on my salad dish and glance toward Donovan's desk. "Me on that desk, you standing, my legs wrapped around your waist."

I can sense the effort it takes for him not to jump immediately to the task. "As I recall, you mentioned there might be cameras…?"

"As I recall, you didn't seem that concerned about them."

"I'm trying to be considerate of your preferences. I don't care if—"

I cut him off. "If *I don't care* means *I think it's kind of hot*, then I feel exactly the same way."

Chapter Ten

The speed at which I'm up from my chair and being hoisted onto my boss's desk has to be record breaking. If there are records of such events, which I'm sure there's not, but maybe there should be.

Though why bother because I already know Steele and I would dominate.

While he undoes his pants, I scramble to get my panties down and over my shoes, which are staying on because they're buckled, and I don't have the patience for that.

"Ah, that cock. I thought I'd never see him again."

Steele runs a finger across my hole and holds it up for me to see how it glistens. "Your pussy's been crying for him."

That's not all that's crying for him. My eyes are also pricking with tears. I'd always thought there were only two things that touch me—superior organizational systems and five-star dinner menus. Steele Sebastian's cock is now added to that list because I'm definitely touched by that beautiful beast, and I've yet to have it in me.

"Don't torture me, Steele. Hurry the fuck up."

As I've already learned, the man does not take direction. Instead, he licks his finger clean, and I guess I can't really complain because one, it's always super fucking hot, and two, he didn't eat any lunch.

"Mm. Still my favorite taste."

I bend forward to lick the bead of moisture on his tip. From there, I'm tempted to stick the whole thing in my mouth, but he wraps his hand around my neck and lifts my face up toward his. "Before you get him all worked up, I need to be sure you aren't going to run out and leave me. My blue balls ached all night long."

I hear the words that come out of his mouth, but the deeper subtext suggested with his tone is what hits me hardest.

"Steele Sebastian, I think you're starting to get attached."

He doesn't say anything, just keeps his hold around my neck as I wrap my arms around his.

"Don't tell anyone I said this, and if you ever try to throw it back in my face, I'll deny every word." I take a breath then let my words go in a rush. "I'm scared, too."

He blinks, and the grip around my neck loosens. Then tightens again.

I think that might be a sign to keep talking so I do. "I'm not good at social norms. I hate small talk and formalized standards. I'm thorny and easily rubbed the wrong way. Everyone gets on my nerves, even the people I like. *Especially* the people I like. I don't put my heart out because it's invariably stomped on, and frankly, I usually deserve it. So I haven't *tried* with anyone in a long time. Tried anything but sex, I mean. Maybe that's all this will be with us, too, but it feels like it could be something more. Something different. Something unexpected. And who knows—we might hurt each other in the end. One of us might leave."

I take another big breath. "That scares me, but I think maybe that new things—that the *best* things—are always going to be terrifying. At first. Maybe even always. I think I might not mind so much, being terrified, if I'm terrified with you."

He nods. Once. "I don't want to stomp on your heart. But I would like to hold it."

He brings his free hand up to caress my face, and I lean into his palm. My heart is beating so fast, it feels like I've run a marathon, but the knot that usually lives in my chest feels like it's starting to unravel.

"I'd also love to spend time with you, preferably in ways that aren't routine or formulaic. But right at this moment—" He drops his hand from my face.

I follow it down as he reaches for his pocket, my eyes catching on his still hard, still beautiful cock, and I wonder how long I'll have to endure this emotional shit before we get back to what we were doing before. Like, is it insensitive to move it along with a little tug and pull?

When he brings his hand out from his pocket, he's holding a condom, and I'm so relieved, I think I might have to consider marrying the man. Especially when he says, "I really need you to shut up and let me fuck you."

The condom goes on so fast, we'd win another record (if that were a thing). Steele positions himself at my entrance, but before pushing in, he brings his thumb down and presses against my clit.

I'm beyond needing foreplay.

I reach around behind him and grab his ass, and after a brief pause to admire how firm an ass it is, I get focused. "You can rub my clit while you're thrusting."

Then I pull him to me, bringing my hips forward at the same time so that he slides inside.

Mostly slides.

Did I mention the man is hung? My eyes had made the note, but must not have passed that knowledge to my pussy because Steele doesn't make it all the way in on the first thrust.

He chuckles. "Your pussy chokes on my cock too."

The date is over so I don't feel the need to have to laugh at his lame jokes anymore. But I don't have the time to respond with the deserved eye roll, because just then, he drives his hips forward and lodges himself so far inside me that my eyes roll back into my head. "Oh, shit."

It is at this moment that I know I'm fucked.

In every way the word means because I'm certain there will never be another man like Steele Sebastian in my life, and I'm pretty sure I might even be okay with that.

I can't think about it too much at the moment, though, since he tilts his pelvis, withdraws, and shoves his cock in again, driving all thought from my head. "Wow. Has just as much impact on the third thrust."

"Second thrust. I'm not counting the time you choked."

Of course he's not.

He repeats the slow withdraw and shove in, and finally, my body opens for him, relaxing around his cock. Giving him room to move.

He smiles against my lips. "For a minute there, I thought you weren't going to let me in."

For a minute there, I wasn't. "I just needed time to adjust."

He kisses me. Too softly for the dirty sex I'm anticipating. But just as I start to pull away, he wraps his hands in my hair and the kiss turns absolutely nasty. His tongue tangles with mine, our jagged breaths increasing rapidly. "Adjustment time over. Because now this cunt is getting fucked."

I don't have a chance to brace myself before he's hammering into me at a brutal tempo. Throwing my legs around him, I lie back on the desk to take the assault.

"Oh, fuck no." At the speed he's adopted, it's amazing he can still speak. "You have to participate. I'm not doing all the work."

"I'm working." I squeeze my pussy around him.

He squints at me, sweat forming over his brow. "Open your shirt. Give me something pretty to look at."

I unbutton my blouse, slowly at first. Until he punishes me with shallow strokes that don't hit the spot that now bears his name. At which point, I rush so fast to get my shirt off, I lose a button.

When he resumes his tempo, I pull the cups of my bra down and plump my breasts with my hands. He bends over me and licks the tip of one rigid nipple and twists the other with his hand, confusing my nervous system with pleasure and pain.

I let out a ragged moan. "You play dirty."

He tugs my nipple with his teeth and releases the other only to smack my breast with his palm, drawing a whimper from my lips.

"Seems to me you like it."

"You're wrong. I hate it. Don't ever stop."

He's grinning when his hand comes to my throat. "Stop talking."

I do as he says, but only because he makes it impossible to speak, first by occupying my mouth with another bruising kiss that leaves me struggling for air. Second, by rubbing my clit so precisely that I start to come and words lose all meaning, which is a good thing because if I could still talk, I might say something ridiculous about love and always and forever.

Except, just as I'm about to peak, his hand leaves my clit and his thrusts slow.

"You fucker." Ah, look at that. Speech returned.

His gaze is focused past me, on the city view. "Didn't you say something about 'naked against the windows?'"

I see where he's going with this. "'While you choke me from behind.'"

In unison, we scramble out of our current position, which means a temporary loss of his cock as he withdraws, then he helps me down from Donovan's desk. I take the opportunity to lose my shirt completely, and my bra as well. Steele's pants are still on, but he loses his tie and unbuttons his top buttons, and I might never need to see him completely naked because he's so hot looking like this.

I stand flush against the windows, briefly wondering if my tits will leave nipple prints. The glass is cool against my hot skin, despite the June sun, thanks to the indoor air conditioning system, causing them to steeple even more. Steele comes up behind me, and I expect him to flip my skirt up and get right back in. Instead, he unzips my zipper.

"You said naked," he says, as my skirt falls to the ground.

Goosebumps spread across my flesh. I'm completely naked against the windows in broad daylight. It's not likely anyone can see me, but it feels like the entire city is watching. I've never had a partner who pushed me to be this bold.

It's only fair that I push him back. "I said choking me from—"

I don't get a chance to finish the statement before his hands are at my throat. He moves so close behind me, I can feel his cock against my ass, still wet from my cunt. He kicks my legs apart, but it's his fingers that find their way to my pussy, and me without the ability to complain.

"I know what you want." He plays with my clit, teasing it with slow, feather circles. "You can have my cock, but only if you can resist coming while I tell you three reasons why you now belong to me."

He's hedging his bets with this one because I really want to come. Sure, I want his cock too, but forcing me to listen to him list three very possibly nice things about me is a real test of my willingness to explore this relationship. I don't even let Donovan say more than one nice thing about me a quarter, and he's one of the longest relationships I've had.

Actually, Steele is quite clever. He presses gently against my windpipe and bends his mouth to my ear, and despite the fact that all my blood has rushed to my pussy, I think this might possibly be the best and only way to woo me.

"One, I only settle for top notch, and your cock-sucking abilities are unsurpassed."

I start to laugh. *This is the best he has? This is child's—*

The pressure on my clit increases and just like that, my orgasm is back and ready to burst.

Closing my eyes, I will the pleasure away, barely succeeding before the growl at my ear returns. "Two, I've never met a woman willing to try and best me. They're usually after my wallet and they purr and coo and flatter me, hoping that's the way to my heart. And the ones who want to get filthy, demand the money upfront. But not you."

It's the most intimate thing he's shared with me. A previously undiscovered protective urge rises up inside me, and if I wasn't so focused on getting railed at the moment, I might fight to get out of his hold and embrace him.

But then he pinches my clit, and again, my climax threatens to overtake me.

"Three. After the orgasm I'm about to let you have, you're going to be permanently indebted to me."

Without any warning, and without letting up on my clit, he thrusts his cock inside me, and fucks me at a merciless cadence. My orgasm crests immediately, raining pleasure on my neural system. His hand tightens at my windpipe, preventing air from reaching my lungs for several long seconds. My vision blacks. Stars start to form. My body shakes and seizes and the pleasure turns to a magnificent euphoria that I've never even come close to experiencing before.

I'm so knocked out by the intensity of my climax, that I'm barely aware as Steele's thrusts get faster and uneven and soon he's groaning out my name, his body twitching with his own release.

Immediately, his hand falls from my neck and wraps around my waist, as though he realizes that I'm only still able to stand with his help and the support of the window. He kisses the back of my neck, then leans his forehead against my head, matching his breathing to mine as my pulse settles into a natural rhythm.

When he pulls out of me several minutes later, I turn around to watch him tie off the condom, wrap it in a Kleenex and put it in his pocket.

Surprisingly considerate. As though he actually cares and remembers that this space isn't my own.

Fuck. I'm going to have to keep him too, aren't I?

"I have more of those," he says, gesturing to the condom. "I think you also mentioned something about on the sofa, you riding me."

"'Tits bouncing,'" I confirm.

He holds out his hand, an unspoken offer to escort me to the couch. My eyes glance past him to the rollaway table and the untouched plate of steak tartare that I'm once again missing on his behalf. If I get to it right now, it might still be edible.

When I look back at him, I give him my hand.

Sex with Steele trumps a divine meal, but only just barely. Obviously, he's going to have to owe me.

Epilogue

Six weeks later

"...and that's how all the meetings in your database automatically get entered on the calendar." I roll the chair away from the desk and stand up so Claudette can reclaim her seat.

"That's absolute magic." She sits down and looks at me with gratitude in her eyes. "But you know you don't have to exchange information with me every time you want to be worked into Steele's schedule. He put you on his 'Always Priority' list."

"No, I really do." She doesn't get how Steele and I work, but nobody does. And that's okay.

I look at my watch. "His next meeting's in an hour, right?"

"Yep."

"Good." I told Donovan I was taking a long lunch. If I stick to Steele's schedule, I should make it back just before his afternoon starts.

Probably.

I stop in the restroom before heading into his office to put on lipstick that will only be smeared off and make sure my hair is extra ready to be pulled.

Then I head into his office, without bothering to knock. "Steele Sebastian, I have a bone to pick with you."

He's in his armchair this time, reading something that's probably important. As usual, he doesn't glance up until he's ready, knowing that every second he makes me wait just makes me wetter. "I believe I've mentioned this before, but it seems to bear repeating—I only see people by appointment."

Ignoring the interruption, I stride forward and put my heeled foot on the coffee table in front of him. I might lift my skirt a little too, enough so he can see just a flash of the goods. "I had an interesting encounter this morning."

"Oh?" He's pretending he's not looking at said goods, but he definitely is.

"Let me set the scene for you—I'd just gotten out of the shower and was about to get ready for work." I don't *officially* live with Steele, but only because he and I don't *officially* do anything. Half of my belongings have made their way over to his apartment over the last month, and I sleep there more nights than I don't. Even when I'm already at his place, he makes every sleepover transactional. Or I do, depending on who happens to owe who at the moment.

I clearly have more to say, but he interrupts. "You still do that?"

"I still do."

"Seems you do it real well too, seeing how you're here in the middle of the workday instead of behind your desk, where you belong."

I don't let him deter me. "As I was saying, I knew Mindy was getting groceries, so I was scurrying around in just my panties. Took me fifteen whole minutes to find my bra."

"Where was—?"

Annoyed with his interruptions, I interrupt him. "The guest bath tub." I pause to remember the antics that got us to that location last night. The look on his face says he's recalling it too. "Anyway, I hadn't had a chance to put it on yet when I walked out into the hall and bumped into a woman who introduced herself as Lola."

His eyes light up. "Lola's back?" He considers for a minute. "I thought she had another week. Guess I lost track of time. Wonder what distracted me?"

I beam because I'm one hundred percent the distraction.

"I was about to call the police, you know. Or at least the front desk, until she explained who she was and that she's been off work for the last two months because she had breast reconstruction after surviving stage two cancer. You asshole. You led me to believe you were paying for her to get a boob job."

"Technically, she did get a boob job, and I did pay." He gives me a naughty grin. "How'd they look?"

"Pretty good, actually. She apparently shows everyone, and so we compared since mine were already out and all."

"If they're better than yours, I can pay for you to have a boob job as well."

It's hard but I manage not to laugh.

Forcing a scowl instead, I climb onto his lap, spreading my legs so my knees rest outside his thighs. "Good job seeing that lie through until the very end. But now you know you owe me."

"Another spanking?"

"This time I think I'd like to spank *you.*"

I'm half afraid his masculinity won't be able to take it. The man is kinky, but he's also in charge.

The other half of me isn't at all surprised when he says, "How about we make a deal?"

Before he even delivers the terms, I'm smiling.

I truly do still hate most everyone, but my list of those I don't has expanded.

1. Donovan

2. Most of his business partners.

3. My neighbor, Ashish (who still waters my plants in exchange for the password to my Netflix account now instead of sex)

4. Doug of Doug's Diner (who still doesn't know I exist)

5. And one dirty, filthy billionaire.

* * * *

Also from 1001 Dark Nights and Laurelin Paige, discover Slash, The Open Door, Dirty Filthy Fix, Falling Under You, and Man For Me.

Sign up for the 1001 Dark Nights Newsletter
and be entered to win a Tiffany Key necklace.

There's a contest every month!

Go to www.1001DarkNights.com to subscribe.

**As a bonus, all subscribers can download
FIVE FREE exclusive books!**

Discover 1001 Dark Nights Collection Ten

DRAGON LOVER by Donna Grant
A Dragon Kings Novella

KEEPING YOU by Aurora Rose Reynolds
An Until Him/Her Novella

HAPPILY EVER NEVER by Carrie Ann Ryan
A Montgomery Ink Legacy Novella

DESTINED FOR ME by Corinne Michaels
A Come Back for Me/Say You'll Stay Crossover

MADAM ALANA by Audrey Carlan
A Marriage Auction Novella

DIRTY FILTHY BILLIONAIRE by Laurelin Paige
A Dirty Universe Novella

HIDE AND SEEK by Laura Kaye
A Blasphemy Novella

TANGLED WITH YOU by J. Kenner
A Stark Security Novella

TEMPTED by Lexi Blake
A Masters and Mercenaries Novella

THE DANDELION DIARY by Devney Perry
A Maysen Jar Novella

CHERRY LANE by Kristen Proby
A Huckleberry Bay Novella

THE GRAVE ROBBER by Darynda Jones
A Charley Davidson Novella

CRY OF THE BANSHEE by Heather Graham
A Krewe of Hunters Novella

DARKEST NEED by Rachel Van Dyken
A Dark Ones Novella

CHRISTMAS IN CAPE MAY by Jennifer Probst
A Sunshine Sisters Novella

A VAMPIRE'S MATE by Rebecca Zanetti
A Dark Protectors/Rebels Novella

WHERE IT BEGINS by Helena Hunting
A Pucked Novella

Also from Blue Box Press

THE MARRIAGE AUCTION by Audrey Carlan
Season One, Volume One
Season One, Volume Two
Season One, Volume Three
Season One, Volume Four

THE JEWELER OF STOLEN DREAMS by M.J. Rose

SAPPHIRE STORM by Christopher Rice writing as C. Travis Rice
A Sapphire Cove Novel

ATLAS: THE STORY OF PA SALT by Lucinda Riley and Harry
Whittaker

LOVE ON THE BYLINE by Xio Axelrod
A Plays and Players Novel

A SOUL OF ASH AND BLOOD by Jennifer L. Armentrout
A Blood and Ash Novel

START US UP by Lexi Blake
A Park Avenue Promise Novel

FIGHTING THE PULL by Kristen Ashley
A River Rain Novel

A FIRE IN THE FLESH by Jennifer L. Armentrout
A Flesh and Fire Novel

Discover More Laurelin Paige

Slash: A Slay Series Novella

Camilla Fasbender has a secret.

Underneath her posh accent and designer clothes lies the evidence of her pain.

Every heartbreak, every bad day, every setback has left a scar.

From behind her camera, she shows the world what to see. And it isn't her.

Until *him*.

He sees right through her carefully constructed facade.

And he's going to slash it all to pieces.

* * * *

The Open Door: A Found Duet Novella

I knew JC was trouble the minute I laid eyes on him.

Breaking every rule in my club. I never forget how he made me feel that night. With all the women in that room, all those bodies on display, but his eyes were only on me.

Of course I married him. Now years have passed. Kids have been born. We're still in love as always, and the sex is still fantastic...

And yet, it's also not. Like many who've been married for a while, I long for the high intensity of those days of the past.

I've heard rumors for years about the Open Door. An ultra-exclusive voyeur's paradise. A place to participate in—or watch—any kind of display you can imagine.

My husband's eyes would still be on me. And maybe other eyes too. If that's what we want.

So when an invitation to come play arrives, how could we turn it down?

* * * *

Dirty Filthy Fix: A Fixed Trilogy Novella

I like sex. Kinky sex. The kinkier the better.

Every day, it's all I think about as I serve coffee and hand out business agendas to men who have no idea I'm not the prim, proper girl they think I am.

With a day job as the secretary to one of New York's most powerful men, Hudson Pierce, I have to keep my double life quiet. As long as I do, it's not a problem.

Enter: Nathan Sinclair. Tall, dark and handsome doesn't come close to describing how hot he is. And that's with his clothes on. But after a dirty, filthy rendezvous, I accept that if we ever see each other again, he'll walk right by my desk on his way to see my boss without recognizing me.

Only, that's not what happens. Not the first time I see him after the party. Or the next time. Or the time after that. And as much as I try to stop it, my two worlds are crashing into each other, putting my job and my reputation at risk.

And all I can think about is Nathan Sinclair.

All I can think about is getting just one more dirty, filthy fix.

* * * *

Falling Under You: A Fixed Trilogy Novella

Norma Anders has always prided herself on her intelligence and determination. She climbed out of poverty, put herself through school and is now a chief financial advisor at Pierce Industries. She's certainly a woman who won't be topped. Not in business anyway.

But she's pretty sure she'd like to be topped in the bedroom.

Unfortunately most men see independence and ambition in a woman and they run. Even her dominant boss, Hudson Pierce, has turned down her advances, leaving her to fear that she will never find the lover she's longing for.

Then the most unlikely candidate steps up. Boyd, her much-too-young and oh-so-hot assistant, surprises her one night with bold suggestions and an authoritative demeanor he's never shown her in the office.

It's a bad idea…such a *deliciously bad* idea…but when Boyd takes the reins and leads her to sensual bliss she's never known, the headstrong Norma can't help but fall under his command.

* * * *

Man For Me: A Man In Charge Novella

Brett Sebastian is the very best kind of friend.

Who else would get me a job at one of the biggest corporations in America?

And hook me up with his uber-rich cousin to boot?

And let me cry on his shoulder every time said cousin blows me off?

Okay, it's pretty obvious that Brett cares about me in a different way than I do for him, but he seems fine with how things are, and our friendship works.

Until one fateful night when I'm mooning over his cousin, and Brett utters four words that should make me happy for him, should make me relieved, should balance out our uneven relationship:

"I met a girl."

Suddenly my world is crashing down around me, and I'm forced to ask myself—am I only interested in Brett now that he's taken?

Or have I been looking at the wrong man all along?

Brutal Billionaire
Brutal Billionaires Book 1
By Laurelin Paige

As the new CEO of Sebastian News Corp, Holt Sebastian has the power to give Brystin Shaw her dream career. But at what cost? Find out in Brutal Billionaire.

He'll get what he wants—even if I'm already taken.

Holt Sebastian is royalty in our world.

As CEO of the Sebastian News Corp, he's the man with all the power. The man who decides if I'll always just be a local television anchor or if I'll be the rising star of my own show.

I make it my mission to be noticed. Make him see my potential. But soon, it's clear he's the one in charge.

His possessiveness is brutal.

His eyes own everything they touch. I feel his gaze on me when he's in the room. The heat of them as they rake down my body, taking me in, marking me as his. He doesn't just want me on the screen—he wants me in his bed.

And Holt Sebastian gets what he wants.

No one will stop him, no one will get in his way.

No one can protect me from his desire.

Not even the man who promised nothing would come between us and his ambition—my husband.

Laurelin Paige delivers a twist on Indecent Proposal in this billionaire workplace standalone romance featuring elements of fake relationship, marriage of convenience, enemies to lovers, and a new alphahole readers will love to hate.

* * * *

"Come on, Brystin. It's a long walk, but it's a short ride. Hop up." Without warning, his hands come down on my waist, directing me where to stand, and even through the thin layer of my tank and the thickness of his leather gloves, I feel heat. The kind of heat that happens low in the belly. The kind of heat that leads to trouble.

Yeah this is a real bad idea.

But considering how I have no good excuse, it's also a bad idea to refuse. Just for different reasons.

"Okay. Sure." He helps me put my foot into the holster, and I try not to think about the way his hands linger on my ass when he helps push me up to the saddle. Instantly, my shorts are riding up my butt crack. "I should have worn jeans."

The comment only draws Holt's attention to my legs, but he misinterprets my reasoning. "I'm sure I'll keep you warm."

"That wasn't. I meant." Do I really want to explain what's happening with my panties? It doesn't help that now I have goosebumps sprouting down my skin. From the attention, not the cold. "Okay."

I'm burning from embarrassment, but yeah, okay.

And then Holt climbs on the horse—not in front of me, but behind me. On a saddle meant for one. "Oh."

"It will be a tight fit." His body practically encases me. His arms come around my center, his thighs hug my hips, and since I'm sure he intended the double entendre, my mind is so completely in the gutter. "But we'll make it work."

Make it work means that I'm pretty much sitting on him. I try to adjust, moving myself forward so that my weight is on my thighs, but he pulls me back against him. "You're good like this," he says. His words are hot at my ear, and he was right—if I was cold before, I'm definitely not now.

"Are you sure? You can't be comfortable." I squirm, trying to somehow make more room.

"Brystin. I'm good." His voice is even deeper than usual. "Trust me."

Then I feel it.

I feel exactly how *good* he is. How blessed he is, anyway, because I'm pretty damn positive that the bulge against my ass has grown. A lot.

All that money and power and God thought Holt Sebastian also needed a big dick.

Life is officially not fair.

About Laurelin Paige

With millions of books sold, Laurelin Paige is the *NY Times*, *Wall Street Journal*, and *USA Today* Bestselling Author of the Fixed Trilogy. She's a sucker for a good romance and gets giddy anytime there's kissing, much to the embarrassment of her three daughters. Her husband doesn't seem to complain, however. When she isn't reading or writing sexy stories, she's probably singing, watching *Billions* and *Succession,* or dreaming of Michael Fassbender. She's also a proud member of Mensa International though she doesn't do anything with the organization except use it as material for her bio.

You can connect with Laurelin on Facebook at www.facebook.com/LaurelinPaige, Instagram @thereallaurelinpaige, or Tik Tok @laurelinpaige. You can also visit her website, www.laurelinpaige.com, to sign up for e-mails about new releases.

Discover 1001 Dark Nights

MACIE by Susan Stoker ~ ENCHANTED by Lexi Blake ~ TAKE THE BRIDE by Carly Phillips ~ INDULGE ME by J. Kenner ~ THE KING by Jennifer L. Armentrout ~ QUIET MAN by Kristen Ashley ~ ABANDON by Rachel Van Dyken ~ THE OPEN DOOR by Laurelin Paige ~ CLOSER by Kylie Scott ~ SOMETHING JUST LIKE THIS by Jennifer Probst ~ BLOOD NIGHT by Heather Graham ~ TWIST OF FATE by Jill Shalvis ~ MORE THAN PLEASURE YOU by Shayla Black ~ WONDER WITH ME by Kristen Proby ~ THE DARKEST ASSASSIN by Gena Showalter

COLLECTION SEVEN
THE BISHOP by Skye Warren ~ TAKEN WITH YOU by Carrie Ann Ryan ~ DRAGON LOST by Donna Grant ~ SEXY LOVE by Carly Phillips ~ PROVOKE by Rachel Van Dyken ~ RAFE by Sawyer Bennett ~ THE NAUGHTY PRINCESS by Claire Contreras ~ THE GRAVEYARD SHIFT by Darynda Jones ~ CHARMED by Lexi Blake ~ SACRIFICE OF DARKNESS by Alexandra Ivy ~ THE QUEEN by Jen Armentrout ~ BEGIN AGAIN by Jennifer Probst ~ VIXEN by Rebecca Zanetti ~ SLASH by Laurelin Paige ~ THE DEAD HEAT OF SUMMER by Heather Graham ~ WILD FIRE by Kristen Ashley ~ MORE THAN PROTECT YOU by Shayla Black ~ LOVE SONG by Kylie Scott ~ CHERISH ME by J. Kenner ~ SHINE WITH ME by Kristen Proby

COLLECTION EIGHT
DRAGON REVEALED by Donna Grant ~ CAPTURED IN INK by Carrie Ann Ryan ~ SECURING JANE by Susan Stoker ~ WILD WIND by Kristen Ashley ~ DARE TO TEASE by Carly Phillips ~ VAMPIRE by Rebecca Zanetti ~ MAFIA KING by Rachel Van Dyken ~ THE GRAVEDIGGER'S SON by Darynda Jones ~ FINALE by Skye Warren ~ MEMORIES OF YOU by J. Kenner ~ SLAYED BY DARKNESS by Alexandra Ivy ~ TREASURED by Lexi Blake ~ THE DAREDEVIL by Dylan Allen ~ BOND OF DESTINY by Larissa Ione ~ MORE THAN POSSESS YOU by Shayla Black ~ HAUNTED HOUSE by Heather Graham ~ MAN FOR ME by Laurelin Paige ~ THE RHYTHM METHOD by Kylie Scott ~ JONAH BENNETT by Tijan ~ CHANGE WITH ME by Kristen Proby ~ THE DARKEST DESTINY by Gena Showalter

On Behalf of 1001 Dark Nights,

Liz Berry, M.J. Rose, and Jillian Stein would like to thank ~

Steve Berry
Doug Scofield
Benjamin Stein
Kim Guidroz
Tanaka Kangara
Asha Hossain
Chris Graham
Chelle Olson
Kasi Alexander
Jessica Saunders
Stacey Tardif
Dylan Stockton
Kate Boggs
Richard Blake
and Simon Lipskar